A Lake Beyond the Wind

A Lake Beyond the Wind

a novel by

YAHYA YAKHLIF

Translated by May Jayyusi
and Christopher Tingley

INTERLINK BOOKS
An imprint of Interlink Publishing Group, Inc.
NEW YORK

First published in English 1999 by

INTERLINK BOOKS
An imprint of Interlink Publishing Group, Inc.
99 Seventh Avenue • Brooklyn, New York 11215 and
46 Crosby Street • Northampton, Massachusetts 01060

Originally published in Arabic as *Buhayra wara'a al-rih* by Dar Al-Adab, Beirut, 1991
This translation was prepared by PROTA, Project of translation from Arabic Literature, founded and directed by Salma Khadra Jayyusi.

Library of Congress Cataloging-in-Publication Data

Yakhlif, Yahyá,
[Buhayra warā 'a al-rīh. English]
A lake beyond the wind / by Yahya Yakhlif ; trans. by May Jayyusi and Christopher Tingley.
p. cm.
ISBN 1-56656-301-1—(pbk. : alk. paper)
1. Arab-Israeli conflict—Fiction. I. Jayyusi, May. II. Tingley, Christopher. III. Title.
PJ7874.A36B813 1999
892.7'36—dc21

98-41185
CIP

Printed and bound in Canada
10 9 8 7 6 5 4 3 2 1

Cover painting: by Fuad Mimi, courtesy of The Royal Society of Fine Art, Jordan National Gallery of Fine Arts, Amman, Jordan.

A Lake Beyond the Wind

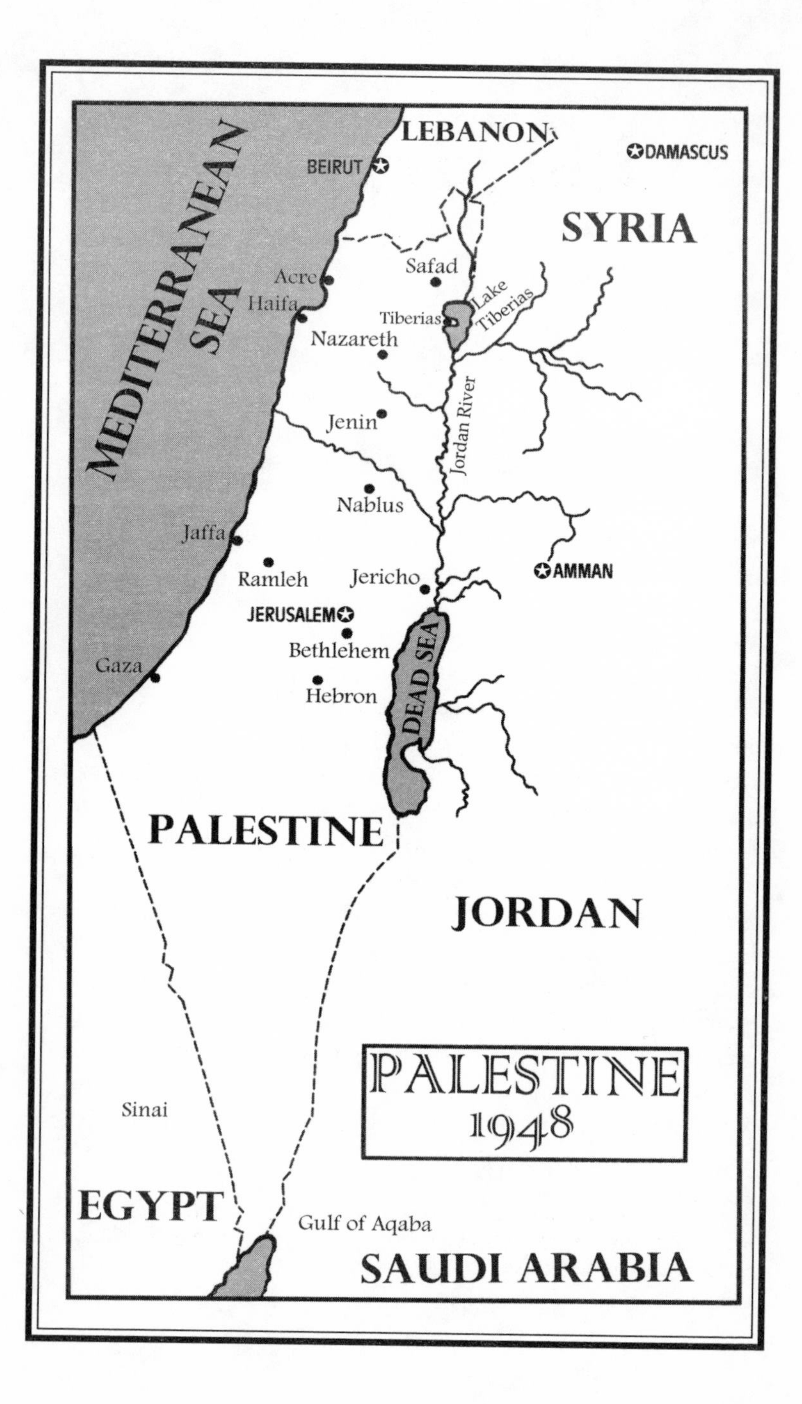

MEDITERRANEAN SEA
LEBANON
BEIRUT
DAMASCUS
SYRIA
Safad
Acre
Haifa
Tiberias
Lake Tiberias
Nazareth
Jenin
Jordan River
Nablus
Jaffa
Ramleh
Jericho
AMMAN
JERUSALEM
Bethlehem
DEAD SEA
Gaza
Hebron
PALESTINE
JORDAN
PALESTINE
1948
Sinai
EGYPT
Gulf of Aqaba
SAUDI ARABIA

Chapter One

Samakh, the South Shore, 1948

Radi sat in his uncle's shop, behind the plumbline scales. As he waited for his uncle to come back, he sold a few things but mostly he was just bored. People in Samakh didn't really know what to do with themselves. They were waiting—waiting for the unknown. The whistle of the Haifa-Deraa train didn't sound now. There was nothing to fill the space of the small town except anxiety; nothing, any more, to evoke a sense of security.

His uncle, Abd al-Karim, had started opening old account books again, searching out hopeless or doubtful debts, trying to collect what he could here and there. He didn't go to Tiberias anymore to buy new stock. He'd been there two weeks before but come back in a panic at midday. Tiberias was a powder keg, he said. Ready to explode at any moment.

In the evening the men sat in the shop fronts, stricken with fear by the broadcasts from the Near East station. "You townspeople," said Haj*

* *Haj*: An honorific title showing that the man in question has performed the *Haj*, or pilgrimage to Mecca, one of the five holy duties of every Muslim. The female equivalent is *Hajjeh*.

Mahmoud, leader of the fighters in the 1936 rebellion, "had better start digging trenches. There are dark days ahead."

At nightfall the darkness grew blacker still. People started whispering, asking one another what they should do. Then there was silence. Silence and anxiety.

In the evenings the men huddled together at the threshold of the guesthouse, their faces pale, as though pinched by cold. They talked of last year's troubles, and the troubles of the present one —another cruel year, with a merciless winter; an outpouring of God's wrath, and days filled with bitterness still to come.

Radi joined the group, staying close to his father Haj Hussein, feeling the deep, surging unease of the white-bearded old man as he rolled his homegrown tobacco in the Ottoman paper, licking the edge of the paper, then smoothing it down and lighting it.

Khaled al-Zaher made the rounds with glasses of tea. He was a shepherd, and he lived in the stables where the seeds and straw and plowshares were kept, along with various other old odds and ends, and where swallows and lizards and spiders made their home.

Coffee wasn't ground in a mortar anymore. And, since the latest round of troubles, all talk of harvest and the calves to be born in spring had given way to talk of the Jews, who'd started drilling behind the settlement of Degania and blocked the road whenever they felt like it. The men no longer told tales of hyenas and foxes and jackals. All the talk revolved around the coming days, whose terrors would turn the blackest hair white. Even the sparrows sensed the fear and, shunning the wide open spaces, settled on the telephone lines.

A disaster was coming and there was a sense of the earth starting to tremble. Around this time, the time of siesta, the trees and the wind fell silent. Even the waves of the lake were still.

It was like the silence and stillness before an explosion at the stone quarries.

Suddenly, standing there at the door, was a fair-haired soldier with a bag on his shoulder; one of those wandering British soldiers who were passing through more often these days, on the way from Jisr al-Majami camp to Haifa, loitering along the way to sell some stuff or buy cigarettes and chewing gum.

There he was. He seemed to hesitate for a moment, but in he came, then stood there without a word. Radi asked if he wanted anything. The soldier looked back, as if to make sure no one could see him, then put down his bag.

Radi felt an instinctive unease, but the soldier made a reassuring gesture. "I've got something worth selling here," he said. "Are you interested?"

Radi pushed the scales to one side. "What is it?" he asked.

The soldier pulled something out of the bag: a vest, navy blue. It was broad and puffed out, with big front pockets.

"This is a real protective jacket," the soldier said. "A bullet-proof vest, lightweight. It's got small plates inside reinforced with fiber-glass."

He held it up for Radi to see. But—what in heaven's name was it?

A bullet-proof vest a man could put on over his clothes, a vest tied at the back and hugging the chest so no bullet could get through to the heart.

"It's really useful for a fighter," the soldier said. "Something special. My mother sent it to me from London," he went on. "As I said, it's something special. She was afraid I'd be killed and this was the only thing she could find to protect me. Apart from her prayers."

Radi gazed, dazzled, at this thing that was so supple and beautiful.

"It's to be worn on top," the soldier said. "If a man wears one of these he won't be killed, and he'll really impress people too."

Radi was duly impressed, and the soldier kept egging him on.

"Have a look at it yourself. Shoot at it and see how strong it is."

Radi wasn't sure what to say or do, and the soldier probably noticed his uncertainty. "My tour of duty's over," he said. "I'll be in Haifa soon, then I'm going home. Look, I'm in a hurry. I'll sell it to you cheap."

Radi was thinking. Of the money in the drawer perhaps.

"I'll make you a good price," the soldier insisted. "Just twenty guineas."

Radi's eyebrows shot up in surprise. A car horn blared outside. Obviously someone was waiting for him.

"You can have it for ten guineas. Here."

Radi thought for a moment of his uncle, Abd al-Karim, who left him in charge of his shop when he wasn't there. Would his uncle be pleased or not, he wondered? Then he put his apprehension aside, took out the ten guineas and handed them to the soldier in exchange for the vest.

The soldier went out, then left in the car. It had all happened so quickly Radi was only now getting back his sense of reality. This thing had happened—the soldier coming in—then leaving. How had he dared spend all that money without consulting his uncle?

The vest was on the table, navy blue, its puffed-up front moving gently underneath the scales. It was light. It looked like one of those suits of armor the old warriors had worn to ward off sword thrusts or piercing spears.

Radi kept gazing at it, bracing himself for his uncle's storming rage when he returned. He took the vest down, put it in a corner away from prying eyes, then sat down to think.

When it came to buying eggs or a chicken, or even making a deal over a measure of wheat, he was authorized to handle things. If it had been a matter of a second-hand bed, or an old carpet, it would have been easier still. But to buy a military vest—that was sheer madness!

A storm of dust swept through the empty square in front of the shop, the square which, on Fridays, became a market for sheep and birds. The leaves were still flying about when Mansour, the ticket seller at the train station, came in to buy a pack of cigarettes. He greeted Radi and held out the money. He didn't need to ask for the pack, because he always ran out of cigarettes around this time of the day. He was wearing a navy blue uniform with brass buttons, and when he talked his smart false teeth showed from behind his lips.

Radi handed him a pack of Yater, and he took out a cigarette and lit it. Then he raised his head, and his eyes focused on the vest.

"What's that?" he asked. He knew something was up. "By God, what is it?" The vest had aroused his curiosity.

"It's a bullet-proof vest," Radi said.

"Where did you get it?"

"I bought it today. A British soldier just passed through. He sold it to me."

"How much did you pay for it?"

"Ten guineas."

Mansour raised his eyebrows. "That's incredible," he said. "It's worth a lot more than that."

"He was in a hurry and sold it cheap."

"Let me have a look at it."

Mansour went around to the back of the counter, then kneeled down to examine the navy blue vest, while Radi watched his reactions.

Astonishment was written all over the ticket-seller's face.

"You're a lucky guy," he said wonderingly. "Make sure you let everyone know before your uncle gets back."

Radi felt a great sense of relief. Mansour adjusted the cap on his head, then went out in his brass-buttoned uniform, back to the deserted station.

✖

A butterfly landed on the sticky flytrap hanging from the ceiling and struggled vainly to free itself. Radi popped a candy in his mouth, leaving it to melt slowly, determined not to look at the dazzling vest. He was still thinking, in spite of everything, of the moment his uncle would come. Najib the fisherman, whose clothes reeked of fish and the salt sea, came in. He usually bought what he needed on credit, and Radi's uncle Abd al-Karim wasn't too keen on him because he was always late settling his accounts. The man was lazy and besides, on top of that, had divorced his wife Badriyyeh, a relation of Abd al-Karim's.

He came in and greeted Radi, then let his eyes wander around the store. Radi got ready to refuse him credit, but instead Najib sat down without a word.

Customers with time on their hands often took a seat like that, but Najib seemed worried and preoccupied. Then he let out a suppressed sigh from his broad, sinewy chest, in a way Radi wasn't used to. Radi relaxed, feeling sympathy for the weary face, whose right temple was lit up by the sunshine now, the first gray hairs thrown into relief.

Najib gazed unseeingly at the square opposite, then said: "When's al-Taher coming back?"

Al-Taher—al-Taher—everyone asked the same question, and no one knew. Some said he'd been seen in the Yasmin quarter of Nablus, others that he'd been seen at the walls of Jerusalem, at Herod's gate. Still others said he'd reached Gaza on his way to Egypt.

"Al-Taher's pretty slippery," Najib said. "No one can catch him." He smiled absently, the smile of a worried man. Then he said, as though to himself: "You're the only one who can save me, al-Taher."

Radi thought of asking Najib why he was so anxious, of trying to lighten the burden that weighed him down. The man hadn't, he noticed, taken out a cigarette to smoke. Realizing Najib didn't

have the price of a loaf of bread or a pack of cigarettes, or tea, or sugar, he took a pack down off the shelf and thrust it in his hand.

Najib took it eagerly. "Tell your uncle," he said—evidently surprised by this generosity and anxious to avoid any misunderstanding—"I'll pay everything I owe him one of these days."

"Why are you asking about al-Taher?" Radi asked.

Najib lit a cigarette and blew out the smoke, "I want to join up with the fighters," he said.

Radi knew what was going through his mind. Scores of men were going east, to Quneitra and Qatanna, enlisting in the Arab Liberation Army, seeking out arms and khaki uniforms, dreaming of heroism and courage and medals.

Ahmad Bey had been a guest of his father's for the past few days. He was a commander in the Liberation Army, and he'd come to spread the news and reassure people, as well as looking out for new positions for his forces.

"Has he turned you down?"

"No, but he hasn't taken me either."

At that moment Abu Hamid's car stopped in the square opposite. It was a yellow Ford and it had come back from Nazareth, passing through Saffuriyyeh and the Subeih bedouins on the way. Abu Hamid got out and started untying the rope that held the baggage together on the top.

Najib gazed at the shiny yellow Ford, perhaps imagining himself riding in the back as it tore along the road.

"So you're waiting for al-Taher to come back," Radi said.

Najib nodded. "I need his advice. I'm going off." He made a gesture toward the horizon.

Al-Taher—al-Taher. That bold adventurer, addicted to wandering and reckless courage, cleaving his way through the heart of the fire, riding difficulty and danger.

"If Ahmad Bey turns me down," Najib said, "I'll just go to al-Kawuqji. They need more men."

His eyes roamed over the shop, stopping suddenly at the vest.

"What's that, Radi? What on earth's that thing there?"

Radi had known the vest would stir his imagination and wake a burning curiosity in him.

"It's a sort of armor, that's all," he said.

"What do you mean, armor. Be serious, will you?"

"I am being serious. It's an armor against bullets."

"Where did your uncle get it?"

"I'm the one who bought it, not him."

"How? Tell me, by God."

"I bought it from a British soldier. He was passing through."

"Can I take a look at it?"

Without waiting for any reply, he went to the back of the store, and Radi let him examine it closely. He turned it over and gazed at it long and hard, then placed it against his chest. Perhaps, for an instant, he imagined himself a warrior. Then he put it back where it had been before.

"What are you going to do with it?" he asked. "Sell it?"

"I don't know. That's up to my uncle."

Najib stood motionless. Then he walked off before stopping once more and giving the vest a final glance. "That armor deserves a brave fighter in it," he said. "Someone who'll be worthy of it. Tell your uncle that. Don't forget to tell him what I said."

He spoke proudly, as though talking about himself.

✖

Khaled al-Zaher stopped in front of the store, reining in the horse that was pulling the cart. "Come on," he shouted.

Radi was still waiting for his uncle to come back, fighting off his feelings of drowsiness. The *muezzin* was announcing the evening prayer.

"Come on," Khaled al-Zaher called again, louder this time.

He was a stableman and servant but a member of the family too. Occasionally he worked as a plowman as well, but he had the authority to give orders and stop people doing things.

Radi yawned, stuffed a few candies in his pocket and got up. The vest was right there in front of him, shrouded by the early dusk, but he would have been able to see it even with his eyes closed. He could see it, sense its metallic feel, even without touching it. He thought for a moment of taking it home with him, then decided to leave it there.

He opened the drawer, tied the money up in a bundle and thrust it down into his chest. Then he closed the door of the shop and climbed into the cart, which started swaying left and right as the tiring horse pulled it.

"The horse is hungry," Radi said. "Why haven't you fed it?"

Khaled al-Zaher was wrapping his head in a black *kaffiyyeh.* *

"I fed it an hour ago," he answered. "It's getting greedy."

Khaled treated animals the way he did humans. He was compassionate with them, and he'd keep them clean and take care of their hooves. Though some animals were disobedient, he never whipped them.

Radi offered al-Zaher a candy, which he put in his mouth as the cart swayed on, down the alleys and around bends.

"Your uncle isn't back yet," al-Zaher said. "Maybe he couldn't collect his debts. Times are hard, and people don't like getting their wallets out."

Sleep crept in on Radi. He closed his eyes.

"And if anyone did open his wallet," Khaled al-Zaher went on, "then it would be to buy an Ottoman rifle. The one with the long barrel."

Radi was too sleepy to pay any great attention.

"Haj Hussein told me he wanted to buy a rifle. He might sell a cow for that."

---

* *Kaffiyyeh*: Large black and white or red and white square headgear worn by men, kept on the head by a band.

Radi leaned his head on al-Zaher's shoulder, unable to fight off sleep any longer. Al-Zaher stopped talking and, tugging on the halter, prodded the horse on.

✖

At the gate the dog started barking and wagging its tail, and Radi, realizing he was home, opened his eyes. Khaled al-Zaher got down to open the big gate leading to the stables, while Radi jumped off and crossed the spacious courtyard to the stairs that led up to the attic.

His mother, her head covered by a white headdress, was lulling his small brother to sleep, and gestured to him, as he entered, not to make any noise. He went in on tiptoe, without a word, took out the bundle of money and laid it in her lap. She nodded her head, then went on rocking the baby, whose white skin was suffused with a rosy pink. He was asleep, with his eyelids half-closed and a smile on his lips. He smiled, his mother said, because a gazelle was passing through his dreams.

He sat down on the mat, waiting for her to finish so he could tell her about the vest he'd bought that day. He wanted to see how she reacted when he told her. Who else, after all, would be able to face his uncle?

He kept quiet even so, and the baby, sleeping now, went on smiling as though a whole herd of gazelles were grazing in his dream. Still Radi waited, then, when he tried at long last to speak, she motioned to him to go out and come back later when the baby was really fast asleep.

He went down into the courtyard where Khaled al-Zaher had untied the horse, hanging a sack of hay around its neck so it could eat its food, while the dog, called Wolf, sat watching.

Radi made his way to the lit reception room at the other end of the courtyard and greeted the guests, but no one heard him.

The men were all deep in conversation: his father; his aunt's husband, who was the local *mukhtar*, or headman; the Circassian; Ahmad Bey, the officer of the Arab Liberation Army; and an unknown visitor. In their midst lay a rifle with a long barrel, which was the subject of their conversation.

Radi sat down and listened. His father had just rolled his usual cigarette, while Ahmad Bey, his snuff box in front of him, twirled his fair handsome whiskers every now and then and nodded his head.

They were talking about the rifle, which the stranger called "Austrian," only to be corrected by Ahmad Bey, who said it was a Khedive rifle, one of the spoils acquired by the people of Najd in their war with the Egyptians, at the time of the Khedive.

They were haggling over its price. It belonged, it seemed, to the stranger, who was somewhere from Galilee and wanted to sell it because he was hard up.

"It's not worth more than ten guineas," the Circassian said. The stranger insisted he'd bought it for twenty, and Radi's father broke in to offer him fifteen guineas.

The stranger relented and agreed to the price. Then Ahmad Bey butted in. "You can't find ammunition for this sort of rifle," he said.

The deal fell through, and the stranger, taking his rifle, rose in a huff. The Circassian tried to calm him, but he wouldn't listen and left. After he'd gone the group fell silent. Suddenly Radi's father noticed he was there, and the *mukhtar* asked if his uncle had come back from his trip, while Khaled al-Zaher came in to pour the tea and offer it to the guests. Then, because it was turning cold, he lit the wood stove. Ahmad Bey went back to talking of rifles and the ammunition for them, about the different kinds and what they were like: the French ones, the German ones with the long barrel, the Ottoman and the Turkish, and, finally, the Czech one, which was excellent but which you couldn't find ammunition for. Next he went on to talk of artillery, the Tommy gun, the Boaz and the mortar gun, then of machine guns, the Sten gun, the French, the Hotchkiss and the Sidaum. Then he started talking about different kinds of bomb, the Miles and the Salabend. In fact he showed off all his comprehensive knowledge. Everyone was all ears, their burning curiosity aroused. Radi wondered whether to mention the treasure he'd left at the store, but Ahmad Bey was still talking loudly, and the men were listening intently and pressing for more. The fire in the stove burned fiercely, with occasional sparks flying out. Then there was a knock at the gate, and Khaled al-Zaher hurried out to open it. The thread of the conversation was broken by the entrance of Mansour, the ticket-seller at the train station. He greeted the others, took off his shoes and walked in.

He was wearing a cloak with a white robe beneath and the traditional Arab headdress on his head. Out of his brass buttoned uniform he looked like one of the *effendis* of Haifa, lacking only a red *tarboush* (fez).

They made a place for him among the group, and, after the usual greetings and civilities, Ahmad Bey went on with his disquisition, dealing now with TNT explosives and their effects; after which he went on to talk about gelignite, before passing on to anti-aircraft artillery with its different calibers, fixed and hand-held, then to tanks and armored cars, and the different guns they carried, and the length of their barrels.

It seemed to Radi that the men were dazzled, that Ahmad Bey was some prodigy who could work miracles—which was, no doubt, why Ahmad Bey was going into everything in such exaggerated detail. The only thing left for him to talk about was the atom bomb. Then Mansour once more interrupted the flow of conversation. "What about bullet-proof vests?" he asked.

Radi felt the blood rush to his head as the image of the navy blue vest with the puffy front surged up in his mind. Ahmad Bey opened his snuff box and, taking a pinch of snuff, put it to his nostrils and threw back his head so as to take it well in. He wiped

his nose, then, straight away, sneezed once, twice, three times. He'd just prepared himself to start talking again when Mansour beat him to it.

"I bet you haven't seen a piece of armor like the one Radi has."

All eyes turned to Radi, sweeping down on him like a sudden rainstorm. He felt the sweat break out on his brow. Did he dare speak, or should he leave? Then he plucked up courage, or pretended to. "I bought it today," he burst out. "A British soldier sold it to me cheap. I bought it with my uncle's money, and I'm not sure if he'll be pleased or not."

His father threw him a reproving look, "Why didn't you tell us when you came in, son?" he said.

Radi scratched his head and said nothing. "I've seen it with my own eyes," Mansour said. "It's really something. If a fighter's wearing that, all the bullets in the world won't pierce his chest."

Ahmad Bey seemed to need another pinch of snuff to take it all in. Then, after just a single sneeze, he said: "What's that? Do you really mean it?"

"I saw it with my own eyes," Mansour broke in. "I swear it!"

Radi's eyes moved from one person to another: his father, the amazement showing in his face; the Circassian, whose face had turned redder; his aunt's husband, who couldn't be moved by an earthquake even; Mansour, flushed with pride at the attention he'd managed to arouse. As for Ahmad Bey, he kept on shaking his head, then said:

"Right. Let's see this vest and make up our minds about it."

Once again they all turned their gaze on Radi. No one had noticed he was there earlier, but now, knowing himself the center of attention, he felt even prouder than when the schoolmaster had appointed him class prefect.

He glanced at his father; and, seeing his father's sympathetic eye on him, felt the old man's tenderness toward him to be as vast as the lake.

"Go back with al-Zaher," his father said, handing him the silver-hilted dagger to protect him in the small town's lonely alleys, "and fetch the vest from your uncle's shop."

Radi got up at once, hanging the dagger at his side. As he was about to cross the threshold, his father added: "Take Wolf with you."

Wolf was still sitting in the courtyard, but the moment he heard his name he sprang up, cocking his ears. He really was like a wolf, always alert and ready for any signal to race the wind.

Khaled al-Zaher harnessed the horse, which looked livelier after its meal, while Radi sat down next to him, carrying a lantern that threw off some of the darkness. Al-Zaher tightened the reins, and this time the cart moved off more smoothly. The horse, its hooves deep in mud, was pulling strongly now, while Wolf sometimes raced in front of the cart and sometimes walked alongside it. When the cart reached the main road, the horse started trotting on the paved surface, while, here and there, municipal sentries blew the odd whistle to show that they were there and all was well.

The night guard in front of the police station was wrapped in a thick coat, and he'd lit a fire to chase away the cold and loneliness. Far off, in the distant plains, they heard a howling that send a shudder through them.

The cart came to a halt in front of the store. Radi got the vest and locked up again, while the dog leaped up in the air and frogs croaked nearby. As Radi was about to climb back in the cart, there was the sound of an explosion, which lit up the horizon. Radi felt himself tremble. Then there was a second, more powerful explosion.

"Get in," Khaled al-Zaher said. "Get in!" He pulled him up, turned the cart around and gave the horse the rein. The horse must have sensed the danger, because it sped off, together with the dog, who wouldn't stop barking.

The horizon, heavy with clouds, was rent by a third explosion. "Oh God," Khaled al-Zaher said, "have mercy on us."

The street was totally deserted now, and no one peered out from behind windows or doors. The cart turned into the narrow alleys, the horse going by instinct. Radi had almost forgotten about the vest. One hand carried the lantern, the other firmly gripped the dagger.

By the time they reached the big gate the explosions had stopped, succeeded by a mysterious, impenetrable silence. Wolf was panting and the reception room was in an uproar. Ahmad Bey, who'd just come down from the roof, said: "There's something happening in Tiberias." Then he added, to himself: "Still, Subhi Shaheen got there a few days ago with his men. It's all under control."

"But there are more Jews than Arabs in Tiberias," the Circassian broke in. The men looked fearful and lost.

"There's nothing to be afraid of," Ahmad Bey answered. "The Arab Liberation Army's getting ready at the borders. The second Yarmouk battalion." He took some snuff. "We'll wipe them off the face of the earth, the bastards."

At this point Khaled al-Zaher came in carrying the splendid vest, and Ahmad Bey, speechless, sprang to his feet.

What power made him stand with such dignity? He took hold of the vest and turned it over, inspecting every part of it, up and down, inside and out. He tapped the metal with his fingers, while everyone gathered around him in awe.

"This really is something," he said. "It's a Bristol-type bullet-proof vest, British made. A superb vest."

Mansour's voice sounded out. "Didn't I tell you?"

Ahmad Bey turned to Radi.

"You did well, son," he said. "How much did you pay for it?"

"Ten guineas."

"I'll give you five more. Will you sell it to me?"

Radi was elated. They were treating him like a man.

He glanced at his father, to draw strength and approval from the old man. His father smiled, then said, "You're standing in for your uncle. Act like a man."

Radi looked at Ahmad Bey in his military dress, at the stars gleaming on his shoulders. Ahmad Bey, he thought, was the one worthy of this vest. He was the knight who could wear it and set off boldly to war.

"Bey," he said, "the money isn't the important thing. What matters is that the vest finds the man who deserves to wear it."

Mansour laughed, and the Circassian cried out: "May God favor you, son."

"You're the one, above all, who should have it," Radi concluded.

Ahmad Bey's face relaxed, and his chest swelled. His eyes gleaming, he pulled two ten guinea notes out of his pocket.

"Here are twenty guineas. Fifteen for your uncle and five for you. You're a brave boy and you'll be a good fighter one day."

Then he picked up the vest and felt its sturdy material.

✖

Najib came in the early morning, beaming and wearing pants tucked into shoes with a high flap and a dark khaki winter jacket. The face that so rarely saw a razor was clean-shaven now, and his thin black moustache made him look younger and more handsome. Where had he found all those clothes? At any rate, there he was. He knocked twice on the door. The gate, through which Khaled al-Zaher had passed with the cart on the way to the pasture near the Karantina, where the flock was, had already been opened at dawn by the old man as he went to pray to the Creator.

Najib crossed the courtyard, which was filled with puddles of rainwater, and came into the reception room whose corner was dripping too.

"Good morning Bey," he said.

Ahmad Bey, huddled in fur, murmured a greeting, and Najib sat down nearby. Najib rarely entered the reception room, where he wasn't welcome, but when he did he knew where the likes of him should sit. Another drop of water fell in the corner.

"All these rains have made the roof leak," Najib said.

The Bey nodded. Perhaps he'd noticed the clean clothes Najib was wearing, because he'd looked hard at the handsome khaki jacket but made no comment. Meanwhile Najib's eyes fell on the bullet-proof vest near the Bey's pillow. "That's a marvelous vest!" he said. "I've seen it before, haven't I?"

The Bey coughed and still said nothing, obviously not wanting to be too familiar with this tiresome man, who never stopped banging on closed doors.

"It's a sturdy thing, isn't it?" Najib went on.

Ahmad Bey stayed silent, but he was only outwardly calm. Inside he was losing patience. It just wasn't proper for this man to keep trying to break down barriers in search of his goal. It was also improper for a would-be soldier in semi-military dress to talk with an officer in his pajamas, whose uniform was hanging from a nail on the wall.

"I bet there's nothing to beat that vest."

At this point the Bey's anger boiled over. He covered the vest with a corner of his fur to hide it from view, then said, in the manner of a military order:

"Stop chattering and go make some tea."

Najib jumped to it, taken aback rather, but pleased too at the recognition reflected in this exchange with him. He searched for some wood in the corner and lit the fire, then he found the sooty kettle, which he cleaned by the threshold. He took some tea and sugar from the box, threw them in the big kettle that was kept over the fire all day, pulled up a cushion and sat down to wait for the tea to boil. In the meantime Ahmad Bey, in a white flannel shirt and coarse woolen longjohns, got up to wash, then went to the toilet in the stables. As the sounds of wind released from the Bey's intestines gurgled like the liquid in a water pipe, the water in the kettle started steaming. The Bey, who suffered from constipation, was making loud popping sounds, and Najib had to fight back the laugh that wanted to come out. When the Bey returned, his face red from the strain, he found the tea all ready in the big glass.

The Bey knew well enough that Najib must have heard the sounds of his struggle in the stables, but he gave no sign whatsoever, moving toward his uniform, which he put on. He thrust his feet into his boots, then, standing erect, seemed a very different man from the one who'd been heaving and straining such a short time before. He issued his second order.

"Now tidy the bed."

In the manner of a soldier who was still a conscript, Najib was happy to obey orders, and did what he'd been told to do straight away. Ahmad Bey sat cross-legged on the mattress, which was actually made up of two mattresses one on top of the other, provided as a mark of respect by the master of the house.

He sat and raised the glass of dark tea, brewed now so that its fragrance spread, while the flames leaped high in the stove. Wolf stood by the door with his dirty shaggy white coat, probably drawn by the smell of the fire. He never crossed the threshold, even by an inch.

Najib looked at the bit of the vest peeking out from under the fur, wishing the Bey would reveal this tempting object, wishing he could wear it one day, the way real warriors did. The Bey drank the glass to the last drop, and Najib poured him another.

"Bey," he said. "Sir. I want to be a soldier with you."

This wasn't the first time he'd made the request— in fact it was maybe the fifth or sixth time, and he'd never received a reply.

The Bey reflected. What was it, finally, that stopped him taking this young man so overflowing with vitality? Why shouldn't this man be his orderly and servant? He seemed obedient and he was burning with eagerness to join the army. But what would the people of the small town say? What doubts would they start feeling if the army took in layabouts who weren't really and truly patriotic?

"Look, Najib," the Bey said suddenly. "Before we can take you, you have to prove you're fit for a place in the army."

Najib poured him a third glass of tea. "Right, sir," he said.

The Bey drank some more tea. "It's war we're talking about, Najib," he went on. "And war needs proper soldiers."

Najib stood up and saluted in his joy. The Bey's words meant he was halfway to being accepted.

The Bey opened his snuff box and took in some snuff, "You must get a testimonial from the mayor or one of the other top people," he said.

"I already have one from the mayor, sir." He pulled a folded piece of paper from his pocket and presented it to the Bey, who opened it and gave it a brief glance.

"Right," he said. "Then, as I'm sure you know, you'll need a physical examination."

"No problem. Can't you see I'm as strong as a rock?"

"And you'll have to undergo intensive training, at the Qatanna base."

"I know that, sir."

"A tough military training that only strong men can get through."

"I know that too."

"As for your wages, they'll be four and a half guineas."

"I want to enlist to defend my country, sir. Not for the money."

The Bey looked closely at Najib to be sure he was telling the truth. "Then you'll be a good, disciplined soldier," he said finally.

A tear almost escaped Najib's eye. Then he said, in a heartfelt voice: "I'll make you proud of me, sir."

Wolf suddenly slunk off as Radi arrived with the breakfast tray.

✖

It was a big tray, laden with food. There were plates of fried eggs, different sorts of cheese, olives, thyme, honey and a pile of hot bread. Radi had woken early, opening his eyes to see a perfectly clear sky and a bird preening its feathers on the window sill.

The heavy rains had stopped, but there were still streaks on the windows, and still the delicious warmth of his bed kept him tucked up inside. His mother's voice had woken him right up, for it was already half past six and he had a lot of chores to do before going to school. His mother had already finished her early morning tasks. She'd watered the flower pots, the basil and the *utrah.** She'd fed the baby and washed its clothes. Then she'd prepared breakfast for the guest, before starting to chat with his aunt across the rooftops.

When Radi came in, Najib, clean-shaven and with clean clothes for once, stood up and, taking the tray, set it in front of the Bey who was sitting there cross-legged in his uniform.

"May God bless you," said the Bey. "You're a good boy."

He picked up a loaf of bread, tore it in two, and broke off a piece, which he then dipped in olive oil and honey and stuffed in his mouth. It was such a big mouthful he could hardly chew it, and, when Najib inquired whether he'd like some tea with his food, he couldn't answer but just had to raise his eyebrows to say no.

Radi sat down alongside Najib, who hadn't dared approach the food. His glance fell on the tip of the vest, and he wished he could see it once more before the Bey left.

The Bey swallowed his mouthful, or rather he gulped it down. It had lodged in his throat, and he would have choked but for Najib, who'd fetched him a glass of water. Then he dipped the second piece of bread in olive oil and yogurt. Before he could put it in his mouth, though, Sheikh Hussein arrived from his dawn prayers,

---

* *Utrah*: A bushy, aromatic plant commonly found in Palestinian gardens.

preceded by his cane and some benign supplications he knew by heart from the book called *The Guide to Good Deeds*.

The Bey put his food aside and made to get up, but the Haj insisted he shouldn't interrupt his meal. The Haj sat down, then asked his guest: "Did you sleep well?"

"Yes, God be praised," answered the Bey. "Won't you join us?" he said, indicating the food.

But the Haj never took anything in the early morning except a cup of the purest olive oil. "May you enjoy your food," he said. The Bey went on eating, while Najib still watched and waited.

"Eat, Najib," the Haj said. "God's bounty is great."

Najib's eyes were glued to the Bey's face. He was anxious nothing should spoil the atmosphere. The Bey made a gesture, an almost imperceptible nod of the head, from which Najib understood there was no objection, and he stretched out a hand and began eating hungrily.

"Haj," the Bey said. "Najib's become a volunteer in the Arab Liberation Army."

The Haj had just taken out his tobacco and cigarette paper. "God shows the way," he said. The words were rather unclear. Did they show enthusiasm or not?

"Najib's brave and strong," Radi broke in eagerly. The Bey looked up at the Haj, who went on rolling his cigarette.

After he'd eaten his fill, the Bey said: "Haj, the country is calling its sons." This meant he'd decided to leave.

"The house is yours," the Haj said. "We're the guests here and you're the master."

"May God preserve the house and those in it," the Bey replied.

He pulled at the fur, to reveal the vest on which all eyes became fixed. Najib looked at it in awe, and the Bey gave him his third order that morning.

"Get moving, Najib. Go and fetch your bag. The car's coming within the hour, to take us to Beisan."

An hour later Abu Hamid's car had set off across the plains. The Bey sat in the rear and Najib sat alongside Abu Hamid, while the vest was with the rest of the stuff in the big suitcase. The car pressed on south, with Abu Hamid scowling and looking neither left nor right, nor in the mirror at the officer who was smoking his pipe non-stop in the back.

"Is it far now?" Najib asked. Abu Hamid merely shook his head in a gesture that meant nothing. Najib repeated the question.

"How many miles now before we get to Beisan?"

"God knows," Abu Hamid answered impatiently.

"Just remember, Abu Hamid," the Bey broke in light-heartedly. "You're talking to a soldier in the Arab Liberation Army. He's not Najib the fisherman any more."

The car was turning a bend that needed all his concentration, so Abu Hamid didn't reply.

"Abu Hamid's a supporter of the Mufti," said Najib jokingly. The Bey shifted a little.

"Then he's a supporter of al-Taher," he said.

Their eyes met in the front mirror, and Abu Hamid broke his silence.

"That's quite true, Bey. I do support al-Taher."

The Bey turned his face away and leaned back in his seat. "Who is this wonderful person?" he inquired.

"He's a son of our home town," Najib answered briefly.

"You could say he is the town," added Abu Hamid.

That put a stop to the one, short conversation that had taken place on the way. The car stopped on the outskirts of Beisan, where between the trees, in front of the military camp, dozens of army tents had been set up in the vast open lands of the Jordan Valley.

✖

The Bey alighted from the car, and the sentry came up with a casual salute.

"Thank God for your safe arrival, sir," he said.

He was a young soldier with a thick moustache, and he had a long-barreled rifle on one shoulder and a rucksack over the other. Around his waist he wore a full cartridge belt from which a water canteen hung. His helmet hung at the back of his neck.

"They're waiting for you inside, sir," he went on. "The Inspector-General's deputy's arrived from Damascus."

The Bey showed a sudden interest. "The Inspector-General's deputy, you say?"

"Yes sir, and a general alert's been sounded through the company."

The Bey's interest turned to embarrassment, which he hid behind a smile. He paid Abu Hamid, while the sentry, along with Najib, pulled out the luggage.

"Be careful with that," he told the sentry, who was carrying the big suitcase. Abu Hamid drove off, and they passed through the gates. After a few steps the Bey turned to the sentry and addressed him pleasantly.

"Asad al-Shahba," he said, "take Najib to your tent and let him stay with you till it's time for him to leave for Qatanna. And take that bag to my sleeping quarters."

He adjusted his clothes, pulled himself erect and hurried off to the company's headquarters.

"This is my tent here," the sentry said. "Or our tent rather." There was no one in any of the tents nearby. "You'll have to stay here on your own," he went on, "until I get off duty. They're all assembling nearby, because of the alert."

Najib went into the tent. It had two beds, one made up with a colored woolen cover, the other bare except for a rubber mattress. He sat down there and laid down his small bag, which had just a few cotton underclothes in it, along with a pair of trousers he thought he might wear if he had the chance to go to Damascus on leave.

He didn't know what to do. The sky was cloudy, but there was no trace of chill in such a warm district. He thought of going for a walk but wasn't sure about it. Finally, tired of waiting, he got up and poked his head out of the tent.

The square was empty. There was a bird, a partridge of some sort, perching on an oleander tree, and a few herbs and plants like fennel and vetch and *khurfeish** were starting to sprout here and there, while, high above, the sky was heavy with clouds.

✖

At the entrance to a nearby tent a man was sitting on a stone writing, with a good deal of jerky movement, like a person bending over a washtub and scrubbing some piece of clothing.

"Peace be with you," Najib said.

"God's mercy and blessing be with you." The man gave the full greeting, though the exhaustion showed on his face.

"Are you new here?" the man went on.

"I've just arrived."

"You're welcome. Sit down, won't you?"

Najib squatted opposite him. The man put the papers in his pocket, striving not to show his irritation. His look, though, said plainly enough: "There are times when it's better to be alone."

"Where are you from, brother?" he asked, putting away his pen. Najib knew from his accent that he was an Iraqi.

"From Samakh."

"Oh. Well, that's not far away."

A military cycle passed by, and the driver, who wore a black helmet and had black goggles over his eyes, waved a hand.

"Don't forget to take the medicine," he called out.

Then off he went, the cycle leaping along the gravel road like a grasshopper. When it had disappeared, the Iraqi laughed.

---

* *Khurfeish*: A common wild plant, with rough leaves.

"That's Adnan," he said. "The medical orderly."

"Are you ill?"

"Just a bit of a chill – that and a touch of stomach pain. Nothing to worry about." He looked weak and exhausted even so.

There was a flash of lightning, followed by the sound of thunder, and before long it had started drizzling.

"Come on," the man said. "Let's get inside."

The floor of the tent was strewn with woolen coverings, and scattered about were cartridge pouches and belts, and cleaning instruments, along with a rifle leaning up against the central pole.

They sat facing one another, as the threads of rain went on splattering the tent. The Iraqi was silent – his eyes were silent, and his face, and even his pallor. Najib was silent too, wishing he could close his eyes and open them to find himself in Qatanna. He was the odd man out among all these trained men. What would he say if this man, with his noble face, were to ask him to help clean the rifle? Or if the conversation turned to the different kinds of weapons, or the arts of war?

The rain was getting heavier now, accompanied by thunder and lightning.

"It's February," Najib said. "You never know what's coming."

Suddenly he missed Samakh. Oh God. Perhaps this man, sitting silently in front of him and clutching a wad of blank sheets, was thinking of Basra or Baghdad, or remembering a house in the outskirts of Najaf.

"What are you writing?"

"Something personal. I'm trying to get something down. You might say, really, I amuse myself by writing."

At that moment the sentry, Asad al-Shahba, arrived, his heavy military clothes dripping with rain.

"I wondered where you were!" he said to Najib. "Has Abd al-Rahman here been treating you to some of his marvelous talk? All his stories and tales, about the wonderful things he's seen?"

The Iraqi laughed. "We haven't had time," he said. "Anyway, he caught me at a bad moment."

Asad al-Shahba took off his wet coat, put his helmet to one side and sat down. He'd just finished his sentry duty and was tired of being on his own. He went on talking and he talked a great deal, about himself, and his hometown of Aleppo, about the training at Qatanna and the military command in Damascus. He described the Inspector-General and his deputy, then went on to tell stories about the troop commander, Muhammad al-Safa, and the company commander, Ahmad Bey. He talked about the Egyptian volunteers, and weapons and military maneuvers, about the Jews—the bastards had started blocking roads, he said—about the importance of reconnaissance, and the settlements and how many people lived in them, and the different kinds of weapon the enemy had. Still he talked on: about the officers and what they were like, their cars, the radio, real alarms and false ones, and the battle there'd be soon. Najib felt exhaustion creeping over him and Abd al-Rahman started yawning too.

That noon Najib slept deeply. In his dreams he saw the lake, and the fields of eggplant, and the lemon and banana groves. He saw the waves crashing on the rocks, and Ahmad al-Mulla carrying water and earning people's thanks. He saw Khaled al-Zaher with the halo of the prophets around his face. He saw the white dog, Wolf, racing the wind to the distant horizon, and the boy Radi asking him about the vest with two tears rolling down from his eyes. The east winds were blowing, bearing the whistling of trains, the roar of steamboats, the din of corn mills, the howling of wolves, and the lustful mewing of cats in February. Then he saw kohl-eyed Badriyyeh, saw her in her nightgown letting down her hair, and it set his body aflame and made his blood run hot. A shell fell somewhere, the sound of the explosion mingled with the sound of groans. Lips closed on lips, and the kiss had the taste of blood. He woke to find himself being shaken violently. He opened his eyes, terror starting from his face.

"Come on, Najib, wake up. Ahmad Bey wants you. You have to report to him right away."

He rubbed his eyes and got heavily out of bed. What a bad sleep he'd had, and what mixed-up dreams! He opened the water flask, drank a little, then wiped his face with some water. He could follow what was being said now.

"The Bey wants me, you say?"

"He wants you right away."

He put on his heavy boots and adjusted his clothes, filled with a sudden sense of awe at the moment to come.

It was a big tent, big enough for ten people, with a folding iron table in the middle. From the top hung an oil lantern, which was lit even though it wasn't dark yet.

The rain had stopped, but the din and turmoil hadn't. There was a constant coming and going within the tent. There were orders, and papers too, as though something momentous was about to happen.

Ahmad Bey sat behind the table, signing papers and issuing orders. The laundryman came in, with an extra heel of mud caked on his shoes. He'd pressed the officer's uniform, which he now hung on a nail in the tent pole. Then an orderly came in, carrying the high black shoes polished right up. Najib stood there motionless, not daring to sit down on one of the many chairs filling the tent. He stood there and waited. The Bey didn't look at him, or address him, didn't even, apparently, realize he was there at all.

So why had he been so insistent he should come? The barber came in with his small case and waited for permission to start work.

Ahmad Bey stood there like a rooster, his hands thrust down in his pockets—thinking. What battle was taking place within this great man?

"Might I be allowed to shave you, sir?" the barber asked.

The Bey threw him a meaningful look. "Can't you see I'm busy thinking?" he seemed to be saying. "How dare you interrupt my flow of thought?" The barber stood there holding his case, and Najib stayed too, filled with a sense of strangeness and awe.

Suddenly Asad al-Shahba came in, saluted and handed the Bey a missive, which he read. Satisfaction and reassurance showed on his face, and his features seemed to relax as the hint of a smile appeared on his lips. "With God's blessing," he said. "With God's blessing." Najib understood nothing, except that the ground he stood on was steadier now, there was more air to breathe and the tension had begun to melt away.

Asad al-Shahba saluted and left, and the Bey now turned to the barber. "Be quick about it," he said, sitting down on the chair, "before we run out of time." The barber sprang to the table, laid down his bag and took out a comb, a pair of scissors, a razor, a napkin, a towel, a piece of soap, a piece of alum, a mirror, and some cotton wool and powder. Then he placed the white towel around the Bey's neck, letting it cover his paunch. He dipped the brush in water and rubbed it across the bar of soap. In an instant lather covered the face of the Bey, who sat haughtily on his chair, his eyes closed in reflection, or out of respect for the razor.

Najib watched the razor as it shaved off the lather and the thick black stubble with it. Suddenly Asad al-Shahba was back with a new missive. He entered and saluted, the Bey turned his head without thinking, and the blade sank into his face. A thin trickle of blood oozed out.

The Bey yelled, the barber became confused, and Asad

al-Shahba took a step back.

"I'm sorry, sir," the barber said. "It was an accident."

The Bey moved his hand to the cut and got a mixture of blood and lather on his fingers. Najib stepped forward and presented a towel to the Bey, who wiped his face, then, ignoring his cut, took the missive, read it and handed it back. "Tell them everything's in order," he said.

When Asad al-Shahba had left, he wiped his face again, but it wouldn't stop bleeding.

"Just a moment, sir," the barber said. "I'll stop the bleeding right away." He hurriedly brought the round piece of alum and rubbed the cut with it. The Bey grimaced as the astringent substance stung him, but still the bleeding didn't stop. Najib stepped forward. "We should fetch the medical orderly," he said, "and let him deal with the cut."

The Bey darted a look at the barber, from the corner of his left eye. "Very well," he said. "Have the orderly come."

The barber departed fearfully, knowing well enough what the Bey's silence meant—that he'd have to pay for his failure on some suitable occasion. The medical orderly arrived and prepared to present himself to the Bey. His trousers were muddy, and he was carrying his first aid bag. The Bey was still sitting in the same chair, having covered the cut with a wad of cotton wool.

The orderly saluted and set to work immediately, while Najib stood alongside him holding the bag.

"Open the bag," he said. He examined the cut. "Ah, it's deep." Fear showed in the Bey's eyes.

"We'll have to put some stitches in, sir," the orderly said. "It needs at least five, but before I do it I'll have to clean the cut with iodine. Heaven knows how many germs there are on that rusty razor of the barber's."

The Bey, his heart sinking, went pale and the sweat poured from his forehead. His eyes wandered around the tent as if looking for help, but there was only Najib there, and the military uniform hanging on the tent pole.

The orderly took out bandages, a pair of scissors, and thread, while Najib stared at the Bey, appalled at all that fear etched on his face. The orderly set to work and the Bey, with a show of courage, submitted. But when the stitching started, he groaned deeply and tried to push away the hand of the orderly, who, well used to this sort of thing, gently pushed the Bey's hand back.

Within half an hour the Bey had a bandage on his face, just under the left eye. With the agitation and tension finally over, he sank back in his chair, while the orderly collected his stuff and requested a three-day leave as recompense for his work.

1800 hours.

The tent had emptied now, and the Bey had recovered some of his composure. It was time for him to get ready.

"Open that iron box," he said. The chest, the kind they bring ammunition in, was in the corner. Najib raised the lid.

"Bring me what's inside."

Inside was the military vest and, alongside it, a black belt from which hung a pistol—a Barbello—in a leather holster. Najib took out the vest and belt and placed them on the table.

What a wonderful vest! Najib imagined himself wearing it, setting off to war. A mere dream, of course. The Bey took off his old uniform, put on the new one, then girded himself with the belt and pistol.

"Come and help me put the vest on."

He wore it over his military uniform. In actual fact it was the vest that wore the Bey. Yes, that was it! The Bey had taken on the awesome appearance of a lion with its mane puffed out.

"How does the vest look? How does it look, tell me?"

The words tumbled from the Bey's lips—and they cascaded around Najib's ears. It was incredible! The Bey was addressing him in a familiar tone, blotting out all distance between them.

"It's wonderful," he said. "Just wonderful, sir."

The Bey seemed to have forgotten all about his cut. He'd started thinking of what he had to do now.

"This is what war's about," Najib thought. The Bey took a few steps out of the tent, followed by Najib.

There was still a patch of light peering from behind the black clouds. A jeep was waiting, with a driver visible in the front and a radio in the back. There was a movement of troops such as he'd never witnessed before. There were military cars standing here and there. There were weapons, ammunition, kitbags, backpacks.

From one of the trucks came the tuneful voice of a soldier singing to the nightingale perched on the pomegranate tree.

"We're off to do our job," the Bey said to himself. "The men's morale is high."

"Let me come with you," Najib pleaded.

"You're not trained yet, Najib."

"I'll carry the ammunition for you, sir. On my back."

"Don't argue, Najib. You'll stay here with the camp guards. Do you hear?"

"As you wish, sir."

The Bey moved off, walking to the car and climbing in without looking back. When the car took off, it was as if the Bey were wrapped around in cruelty, just as he'd been by the vest.

Still Najib stared at the car until finally it disappeared behind the hill, followed by a convoy of military vehicles. Within minutes the place was deserted.

✖

He walked about among the tents. There was nothing around but empty tins, a few eggshells, and some keys from sardine tins. No one but a few guards gathered at the gates of the camp.

He passed in front of his Iraqi friend's tent. There wasn't a trace of the man's rifle and uniform; he'd gone off to the war too. If only he were to return with all the gloom gone from his face, with the light of victory shining in it! There were those papers under his pillow. What was it he was writing? He passed the tent, but didn't go in. Darkness was slowly spreading. He walked around, here and there. He sat down, then stood up. Then, more bored than ever, he went back to his tent. It was night. The heart of darkness. No movement except the beating of your own heart, and the wind that howled with a sound to pierce the soul. The guards had stopped their loud talk, as though they too were weighed down with boredom or sadness. His eyes stayed open in the pitch black. All he could see was the darkness. Like those unsleeping sea creatures in the deep, his eyes stayed open; and like sea creatures, too, endless anxieties surged inside him. Black thoughts struck like fins at the passions of his weary heart.

Alone, Najib, he thought, you're beset by black thoughts. Beset by anxieties. He argued with himself. To sleep or not. Floating in a haze, he slept, or had something like sleep. Was it just jumbled dream or the remnants of fantasy?

The unknown swelled to fill the sky. The cannons echoed. The world shook. The sky burned. Beyond the flaming horizon, the Bey drew his pistol. A cry sounded. A shudder. Blood was spilled. The wind rose. The fighting grew fierce. Guns spluttered. People scattered in confusion, their hearts in their throats. Face to face combat with bayonets. The blade plunged up to the hilt under an armpit. Corpses piled up on the ground. The square was topsy-turvy. The air was full of cries for help and the sounds of burning.

Suddenly he woke, and sprang to his feet in the middle of the tent. He had the feeling, in that darkness, of someone who'd been buried alive and woken after the mourners had left.

What black raven had alighted, on that tree of unbearable pain? He invoked the name of God and recited the *Fatiha*.* He felt in the dark for the jug, drank and wiped his face with some water. His throat was dry. How cruel the thirst of the night was.

The guards were talking loudly once more. Once more they were talking of terrible things, of fires that spring up from mountaintops. He wished the voice that had stirred his yearnings would return and sing to the nightingale perched on the pomegranate tree. He wished he could close his eyes, and open them to find himself by the lake. He felt a desperate need to talk to someone, or for someone to talk to him.

He sat with them, staring into the fire. There were three of them guarding the camp gate, wrapped up in their thick coats, trying to beat the cold and the long night by burning wood and talking of war. They offered him tea and cigarettes, and gave him the latest news of the battle. The target, so the soldier in the signal corps unit had secretly told them, was the settlement of Tirat-Zevi, or Qalat al-Ziraa as the locals called it. The fighters were encircling it at that very moment, preparing to take it by storm.

Second Lieutenant Ghassan, the first guard said, was leading the infantrymen brought from Qatanna before the end of their basic training. The second guard added that Second Lieutenant Sa'doun was leading the bedouin corps who had come in from Hijaz; they were expert raiders on camels and good at fighting with daggers, only not trained in modern fighting skills. And according to the third guard, the third company, made up of Egyptian volunteers

* *Fatiha*: The opening and most repeated chapter of the Quran, recited on happy and sad occasions alike.

mostly, had been assigned a supporting defensive role. This was the only force that was properly trained. Captain Muhammad, the first guard went on, was the leader of the battalion and Ahmad Bey his most distinguished aide. One of the others, responding to this, gave a lengthy prediction of what would happen at zero hour.

O those dire forebodings that set rabid terror loose, leaving it to fill the face of the earth and all its cracks! Suddenly thunder rent the black sky, to be followed, soon, by that fearful light. Within seconds it was pouring and the fire went out. A strong wind blew up, almost bringing the tents down. A cold shudder seized them as they lay there, and still they shivered.

Next morning—1000 hours.
A muddied truck arrived, and some exhausted soldiers got down. Their clothes were muddied too; they even had mud sticking to their eyelashes and the collars of their khaki jackets. They got down without enthusiasm; weary and limp, holding their rifles weakly, as though they were carrying lumps of wood.

The guards sprang up, their soaked coats reeking of naphthalene, to learn the news. The soldiers had returned defeated.

The first soldier had a handsome face, but he looked broken. The second soldier's eyes seemed dead. The third was leaning on his companion's shoulder. The fourth was pale, his face clouded with tears.

"How did it go?"

No one wanted to talk. Some of them just wanted to hurry off to bed, to bury themselves in the depths of sleep. They wanted to sleep deep, or simply pass out.

1300 hours.

A truck arrived carrying the heavy weaponry and shells.

Its wheels had sunk into the red soil, and the driver was barely visible behind the filthy windows.

1400 hours.

A band of infantrymen arrived without their guns, their faces dirty, their clothes and boots torn.

1500 hours.

Ahmad Bey arrived in a rented car. He got out, his face swollen and his helmet soiled. He came forward in his wet clothes, the Barbello swinging from his belt. He was confronted with questions and talk, but he rushed straight to his tent without stopping to give an answer. Najib didn't dare go into the tent, but, as he edged ever closer, he seemed to hear a faint sound of weeping.

Asad al-Shahba spread out his wet clothes and wrapped himself in a woolen blanket. Najib had lit a pile of wood in a container he'd fetched from the kitchen, and when he was sure it was burning safely he brought it into the tent and put it down in the middle. Asad al-Shahba was trembling, either from cold or from the terrors of the night before. Various emotions swept across his face; then he wept.

Najib said nothing, leaving him to find relief from his burden in his own way. He wished he'd talk of what had happened and how it had ended. He wanted to ask him about the Iraqi, Abd al-Rahman, and about the boy who'd sung to the nightingale perched on the pomegranate tree. He wished he could weep like him, or else explode, or fly away. Some embers burst and the sparks flew. Eventually the warmth spread and the clothes dried. Tears dried in the eyes too, and some of the dankness affecting the spirit dried out. Finally Asad al-Shahba was ready to talk.

"The attack on Tirat-Zevi," he said, "started at three in the morning. We encircled it from three directions. It's a fortification, not just a settlement—it's surrounded by watch towers, barbed wire and trenches.

"When the Jews sensed we were getting ready to attack, they opened their water pipes and flooded the fields, so they turned into a swamp. We didn't have the tanks to get across.

"I was given the order to creep over and blow up the watch towers under cover of darkness. It was a dark, wet night, and the moment I set out it started pouring, so that the mud got even worse.

"I had some men with me carrying mines. After a lot of problems we managed to get close to the tower. Then the searchlight was turned on us and the Jews opened fire. We threw ourselves on the ground, down in the mud, and when the searchlight moved away we rushed up to the barbed wire and made an opening. But we were surprised by a trench filled with water. The searchlight had lost us and it was dark again all around. We hadn't known there was a trench there. They didn't brief us on it when they gave us their report from the reconnaissance.

"I threw myself down in the trench. I was up to my neck in water, keeping my hands up high. I finally managed to get across the trench and came out the other side wet through, with the rain pelting me from all directions. I reached the main tower and planted the mine right underneath it. Then I lit the fuse and moved some way off, but the fuse went out because of the rain. I went back and relit it but the rain was so heavy it went out again. I tried a third time, and a fourth, but it was no use.

"It was close to dawn. I was in total despair and let loose a scream from my depths. I implored God to stop that cursed rain. Suddenly there were shots being fired at me. I threw myself on the ground and started crawling. I crossed back over the trench, passed through the hole in the wire and got back to where I'd come from.

"Then the fighters aimed their mortars at the tower and damaged the searchlight. The shelling got fiercer and the tower started to collapse. But the infantrymen, under Second Lieutenant Ghassan, couldn't advance because of the mud and the rain and the ground, so soft it was more like a swamp. The Jews went on with their shelling and machine-gun fire, and a lot of fighters were killed. After these losses we got the order to withdraw, which we did. Second Lieutenant Abd al-Aziz and his troops covered our retreat.

"It was eight-thirty in the morning when the failed attack ended. With my own eyes I saw the corpses strewn all over the swamp, in all directions. And with my own eyes I saw Ahmad Bey withdraw before we did, running off after his car had got stuck in the mud. I saw Samih Haddad swimming in his own blood. I saw Salim al-Bishtawi disemboweled. I saw Zain al-Saidi take a direct hit from a shell and get blown to bits."

Asad al-Shahba stopped talking then. He was choking on the words. In a hoarse voice, Najib asked: "What about the Iraqi? Abd al-Rahman?"

"I don't know," the other man said, in a stricken voice. "I don't know."

1800 hours.

More men staggered in. Najib lit a lantern, which gave out a wan light. Near the bed of Abd al-Rahman the Iraqi was a bottle of medicine. And under his pillow there was a bundle of papers, a lot of papers. Just what had the man been writing? Was it his will?

1900 hours.

A group of men arrived who'd lost their way. Their morale was shattered, and they were seriously wounded. The taste of defeat was bitter; everything was falling to pieces.

2000 hours.

"The Bey wants you."

Najib went without enthusiasm. He entered the tent to find the Bey lying in bed, swathed in several heavy woolen blankets. His face was swollen from the cut whose bandage had slipped off. The cut had been exposed to cold and rain and mud, and the swelling was so great he couldn't open his eye.

He'd flung off his uniform, tossing it anywhere, and was himself lying there in his underclothes. His military boots were lying on the floor, full of mud, and the precious vest, also covered with mud, had been thrown negligently under the bed.

"I want a glass of hot milk, Najib," the Bey said. "Go to the kitchen and tell them to make one now."

Najib was overwhelmed with a sense of sadness, grief, and defeat. He felt pain and tightness in his chest. "Right away, sir," he mumbled.

At that moment someone peered in and said, in some confusion and haste: "The Inspector-General's deputy has arrived, sir."

The Bey drew up the woolen covers as if to hide his nakedness —just in time before the deputy entered. He was very smartly turned out, his uniform pressed and a medal hanging on his chest.

The Bey tried to get up, but the deputy, who'd just arrived from Damascus, motioned him to stay where he was. Najib gathered up the boots and clothes strewn over the floor and placed them under the bed, just next to the vest. Then he went to a corner and stood at attention.

"I bring you greetings from the leadership," the deputy said. "May I congratulate you on your courage, and also offer my condolences for your martyrs."

He approached before the Bey could answer, glanced at the swollen cut in his face, and said: "That's a mark of honor, to commemorate this glorious battle."

"We only did our duty, sir," the Bey answered, regaining some of his assurance.

The deputy took an envelope from his pocket and placed it

under the Bey's pillow.

"This is a small token," he said, "from the the Inspector-General."

The Bey did a repair job on his sagging morale.

"I thank you," he said, "for your faith in me, and for the faith of the Inspector-General."

"It was a glorious battle at any rate," the deputy repeated.

Still covered up by the wool blankets, the Bey gave his answer:

"We taught those bastards a lesson they'll never forget."

"Write that in your report to the Inspector-General," the deputy said with a smile. "And be sure to talk to the reporters. They'll be coming tomorrow with the representative from the Information Department."

"We inflicted heavy casualties on them," the Bey went on. "And we captured military and other equipment."

"Write that in your report," the deputy said again, "and mention it to the reporters."

The Bey, who'd now forgotten all about his defeat, added:

"Sir, we captured a fine military vest, better than any you'll find anywhere."

Najib looked at the Bey in astonishment, unable to believe what was happening. How could the Bey tell such a shocking lie? The Bey leaned over, stretched out his hand and pulled the mud-caked vest toward him.

"We captured this fine vest as booty from the Jews," he said, "along with the other things we took in the battle. There's some mud stuck on it, but it can be cleaned easily enough."

The deputy looked it over, took it to inspect it, then nodded his head admiringly.

"It's British made," he said, giving him a long look. "Bristol model."

"Yes. Bristol model," the Bey answered. Then he added: "I'd like you to take it with you, sir, and present it as a gift to the

Inspector-General. As a gift and memento from his loyal soldiers."

He turned slightly and addressed Najib in a commanding voice.

"Najib, take the vest and put it in the Brigadier-General's car."

Najib felt as though the words had come crashing down on his head. Still, he bent down, took the vest and left the tent. But he didn't stop when he got to the Brigadier-General's car, which was surrounded by several of his attendants.

Instead he went on, hugging the vest to his chest. He passed through the camp without anyone stopping him, and made his way through the drizzle and the cold winds.

He walked quickly, for a long way, in obedience to some compass in the depths of him. The distant smell of the lake kept drawing him on.

Chapter Two

It was a warm morning. The clouds had passed by and a watery sun was shining. In front of the station with its tiled roof squatted a number of children in long white shirts, waiting for the sun to get stronger so they could use the holiday to play with their marbles.

Mansour, the ticket seller, always put his chair in front of the stationmaster's office, which was closed now. He'd turn the chair around, then sit leaning on its back. In front of him, as far as the eye could see, stretched rail tracks passing though farm land—a silent farming district, wide and empty.

Above the orchards a flock of storks, just back from their winter migration, flapped their wings. Every so often someone riding an animal from the surrounding villages and countryside, carrying his grain to be ground at Ishaq al-Shami's mill, would pass by and raise his hand in greeting.

Mansour had unbuttoned his navy blue jacket, and he was holding an old newspaper he'd read before, reading it over again to keep boredom at bay. There was no one else at the station, along whose embankments the wind had whistled all night long. A stone's throw away there was a single installation worker laying pipes, for the municipal project to bring the lake's water to people's homes.

Mansour stayed sitting on the chair all morning, sometimes crossing his right leg over his left, then, at other times, crossing his left leg over the right. Finally, his patience exhausted, he got up to stroll along the empty platform, beside the shiny tracks and the oil patches and the traces of grease.

Finding himself out of cigarettes, he flung the paper aside and went off to Abd al-Karim's shop. He wanted a pack of cigarettes, but he hoped he'd find someone to talk to as well.

Radi was standing by the door of the shop, holding a wire trap of the sort the children used to catch fish.

"You've got a trap, I see," Mansour said. "Are you off to the lake?"

Abd al-Karim raised his eyes from his account book to see who was talking, then went back to the book.

"It's Friday," Radi said. He was wearing a loose-fitting gown and his hair was tidy and well combed. "There's plenty of free time. It's warm down in the lake."

Mansour, who took an interest in everything, looked again at the wire trap.

"You've made it well," he said. "You're a hard worker."

Abd al-Karim, seized by a feverish urge to collect his debts, was still adding and subtracting. He raised his head, took a pack of Patra, handed it to Mansour and, once more, went back to the book.

Mansour took the pack and lit a cigarette. Still, it seemed, he hadn't despaired of gaining Abd al-Karim's attention.

"Did you hear about the battle yesterday," he asked, "at the al-Ziraa settlement? They say the Liberation Army had heavy losses and a lot of people wounded."

Abd al-Karim seemed not to be listening. Radi's interest, though,

was aroused. He put the trap to one side and listened attentively.

"God knows what happened to Ahmad Bey," Mansour went on, "who bought that mighty vest."

Abd al-Karim raised his head at that. Radi asked eagerly:

"Is there any news of Najib?"

"God only knows what's happened to him."

"You mentioned the vest," Abd al-Karim said. He couldn't help himself. "Uh—what happened to it, do you know?"

Abd al-Karim was driven by curiosity about the vest on which he'd made five guineas profit without even seeing it. That great vest, navy blue with big pockets, which protected the wearer against bullets.

"The vest's all right, Abd al-Karim," Mansour said. "It'll come to no harm as long as Ahmad Bey's wearing it."

"What's happened to Najib?" Radi asked again. "Hasn't anyone heard anything?"

"Don't be afraid for Najib, Radi," Mansour said. "Najib has seven lives, like a cat."

Radi said nothing. He seemed sad or lost in thought. Still Abd al-Karim went on asking about the vest, and Mansour, using his imagination, gave him humorous, exaggerated answers.

Khaled al-Zaher arrived and prodded Radi.

"Come on," he said.

He'd stopped the cart some way off, because it wouldn't have been proper to stop at the entrance to the shop when he had Aunt Hafiza riding with him. Radi bent down, picked up the wire trap and walked off without a word, afraid his uncle might remember something and stop him from going to the lake.

His aunt Hafiza, who wore a black gown with a wide sash at the waist from which a bunch of keys hung, was sitting in the front of the cart. Behind her was the goathair tent she set up every spring, on the Duwair hilltop, when fat was collected, and honey and *kishk** and green wheat. She was just raising a hand-rolled cigarette, so he climbed into the cart without waiting for an answer to his greeting.

"Abd al-Karim seems a touch crazy to me," she said, frowning as though she were reproving him and not his uncle. "Does he want to take his money into the grave with him when he dies?"

Khaled al-Zaher pulled at the reins and the cart set off, swaying along, its wheels sending out an irritating screech, as though they were sinking under the weight of the tent—something usually carried only by powerful, patient camels who can put up with any hardships almost. Hafiza was scowling and morose, but it was only a passing mood; she was a good-hearted woman with an even temper. Soon she'd reach the lake, and there, among its open spaces, the clouds would roll off and her smile would shine out.

Soon she'd roll up the sleeves of her dress and wash the tent she took out from the attic at the same time every year. She'd give it the usual vigorous wash, intoxicated by the fragrant breeze that blew in from the lake, from the furthest part of it the eye could reach. She'd be picturing her annual trip to the Duwair estate, where, on the hilltop, near the river and not too far from the oleander trees, the shepherds would set up, under her gaze, the big black felt tent, which was the signal to start the work of gathering produce, taking honey from the urns, churning the milk to get the butter, preparing the *kishk* and shearing wool.

The cart turned into the alleys that led to the shore, passing behind the National Committee building and in front of the Abu Ala café. Then it went down to the jetty and stopped at the cement wall that held back the lake when the waves were high. The aunt got down first, followed by Khaled al-Zaher; then, finally, came Radi holding his wire trap. He went down the stone steps, to the

* *Kishk*: Yogurt, either dried into cakes or powdered for later cooking as the base of a sauce or soup.

jetty that stuck out like a tongue on the sides of the lake.

All along the shore were women washing clothes and utensils, and men strolling or fishing with a line; and there was Ahmad al-Mulla hurrying along with a pole across his shoulders and two pails hanging from it. The sweat poured down his forehead as he carried the clean water to people's homes.

A little way off were a number of boys who'd been tempted out by the warm morning. They were walking behind one another in lines like a train, all over the sandy shore, sending out noises like a train's whistle.

Radi put the trap down by the edge of the jetty and sat there dangling his legs, while his aunt descended to the shore with inimitable dignity, followed by Khaled al-Zaher, who was carrying the tent piece by piece. It was impossible to carry it all at once.

When his aunt arrived, she rolled up her sleeves and lifted her garment just above the anklets. Then she took off her shoes that were like soldiers' shoes, took some bars of soap from a bag in her hand, and went down to the water to wash the first piece. Many women sprang up right away to help her.

Badriyyeh was one of the first, leaving the food utensils she was washing and hurrying to help Aunt Hafiza, and she was followed by the Itit woman, Fatima al-Maghribiyyeh, and Sultana, the midwife and hairdresser.

Radi could view the whole scene from the jetty: the lake, the people, the distant houses and the launches out in the deep part of the lake, some small boats and a solitary kayak going north.

He still had the trap alongside him. He'd worked it tightly and with care, spent many hours twisting the wires, then encasing them in the kind of netting used for chicken coops. It was made in the form of a cage, with a narrow conical entrance. The fish would enter to eat the bait, then be trapped and not find their way out again.

Radi took off his gown and got ready to go down in the water. He'd prepared everything, putting the bait inside the trap and tying a hemp string to it with a piece of wood at the other end. The wood would stay afloat to show where the trap was if the waves swept it out.

He threw the trap in and flung himself in after it. Then he started swimming, pushing the trap in front of him, surrendering to the warm waters below the surface and gliding among the calm waves. The breeze was soft and light, and made ripples and wrinkles as it blew across the face of the lake, which was as smooth as the underbelly of a gazelle.

Still he swam, driving the trap along in front of him. When he'd reached the point he'd fixed in his mind, he glided down like a fish, till the trap settled on the bottom. Then he came up again, holding the piece of wood and the string.

Back on the surface, he took a deep breath of air that was suffused with the scent of lemons from the orchards, and turned back toward the shore, now swimming on his sides, now on his back. The sun rose high in the sky, and there, from his vantage point at the jetty, Radi watched and waited.

The din of Ishaq al-Shami's mills went monotonously on, but it didn't alarm the storks whose return from migration heralded the coming of spring. The whistling children had scattered now, and were playing with the shells and sand. Aunt Hafiza was standing idle while the other women did her work for her, each one rubbing a piece of the tent. Khaled al-Zaher had untied the horse and taken off the saddle and bridle, leaving the animal to go down the earth slope to graze and drink, while he himself went off to the Abu Ala café for a puff on the *nargila.** It was something he didn't do very often, but this was one of the rare occasions he ventured it.

---

* *Nargila*: A kind of pipe in which the tobacco is drawn through water.

Suddenly a glider appeared on the horizon, its presence announced by the drone, and all eyes turned upward. It was one of those amphibious planes that passed over occasionally. It belonged to the border guards and landed on a special platform between floating barrels.

The plane got ever nearer, until the pilot's face, with its black goggles, was clearly visible. It made a loop, then started its descent, and before long it was landing gently over the waves like a wild goose.

Radi watched the scene from his spot on the jetty. He saw the children, who'd abandoned the sand and shells, get ready. The plane had gliders and two extended wings, one above the other. It settled within the allotted area among the red-painted barrels, among the black floaters and iron chains surrounding the cement platform, to which the plane was tied to keep it from being swept away by the waves.

The children waved, then took off their clothes and hurried to the water. They flung themselves into the gentle waves and sped toward the plane, whose pilot usually opened the doors to throw cookies and candies out to them. Occasionally he'd throw coins into the lake, and they'd dive to the bottom to get them.

The children knew what they were doing. At that time of year the surface of the lake was really cold, but the water just below was warm, and they submerged themselves with only their small heads showing.

Still they pushed forward with their arms and legs, exactly like tortoises, nearer and nearer, till they were just a few yards away from the plane. The doors, though, didn't open. The pilot was scowling, while on the rear seat sat an officer whose features couldn't be made out because of the spray on the windows.

The plane was swaying over the waters, pulled by the waves but anchored by the chains. A boat approached, belonging to the border guards, and it stopped the children, who drew back.

When the door of the plane opened, the boat inched its way alongside. Then the officer got out, helped by someone from the boat. He was tall and wore a dark green uniform. When he'd settled into the boat, it sped off toward the part of the shore where the military camp was.

The children went back, panting, to where they'd come from. Then they put on their clothes and started whispering. One of them made a gesture toward the plane and shouted: "Cursed plane!"

"Under the mercy of the sword," the others answered.

Radi laughed from where he stood by the jetty. Ahmad al-Mulla came up with his two empty pails, the sweat pouring off his forehead and the veins in his arms standing out, his face pale from exertion. But still, honest, honorable man that he was, he'd wade out to the deepest point he could manage in order to fill his pails with water as pure as spring water.

Badriyyeh, her duty done for Aunt Hafiza, returned to her place on the shore and went on washing her plates and pots and utensils. Small fish, lured by the smell of food remains, came close, on the lookout for an easy meal. They'd come so far they'd almost leave the water behind; then, at the last moment, they'd instinctively draw back and save themselves.

Badriyyeh raised her dress to keep it from getting wet, exposing two white legs. With a pot in one hand and its lid in the other, she waded a few steps into the water and set up a trap for incautious fish. Within minutes a fair-sized fish went into the pot, drawn by the smell of the food sticking to its sides, and Badriyyeh, with a sudden movement, put the lid on to trap it. Radi laughed again from his vantage point, and Badriyyeh smiled; but she let her dress down too, to cover her legs, because this boy was growing up now.

A picture of Najib flashed through Radi's mind—Najib, who'd once been Badriyyeh's husband. Why not tell her Najib was a volunteer in the Liberation Army now, and that, Mansour had told him that morning, he'd fought against the Jews at the battle of al-Ziraa? Why not—? Suddenly Aunt Hafiza's voice cut in.

"What are you doing, Radi? Go and find Khaled al-Zaher, so he can help us spread the tent out to dry."

His aunt, with her wide sash, looked strong, with the strength to do remarkable things. She was still powerful, still in control, and when she made up her mind about something, you couldn't budge her. Putting his fingers in his mouth, Radi let out a series of short whistles, which he kept repeating.

Just a few moments later Khaled al-Zaher came running. He was panting, even though the distance between the Abu Ala café and the jetty was no more than a few yards.

"It's time you did something," the aunt said, fixing him with a reproving eye. He knew what he had to do without being told. He carried the clean, folded pieces of tent and spread them out on the soft sand. They were really heavy from all the water they'd absorbed. He spread them out here and there, watched by the aunt, who kept nodding her head. The Itit girl was standing next to her, but Fatima al-Maghribiyyeh and Sultana the midwife had gone.

The tent was spread out on the sand now, and the aunt was looking it over. There were the various sections: the right-hand flap with the part assigned as seating space, and there was the part for sleeping, and there was the left-hand flap, for storing things.

Suddenly Radi remembered his wire trap and pictured the fish greedily attacking it, drawn by the smell of the bait. He stood up and got ready to enter the water.

He swam vigorously, paddling with his arms and legs, like a boat sped on by the wind, cutting powerfully through the waves. He searched out the marker, the piece of floating wood, and when he spotted it he dived into the depths of the lake and swam on down following the string. The water was warm, with the sun shining through it, and there at the bottom the fish were flapping in the trap. He shut the trap and pulled it up, trying, as he pushed it in front of him, to estimate the weight of the catch inside. He started feeling a weariness in his muscles, but still he went on swimming.

He reached the shore and lifted the trap out of the water. Most of the fish became calmer, but some went on jumping and struggling. He realized then he'd caught a *balbout*, which can live for hours after leaving the water.

As he raised the trap high in the air, Badriyyeh said admiringly, "God save us from the evil eye!"

His aunt, though, showed no interest. She was staring at the lake—into the far distance, as though moved to sadness by something deep inside her. Khaled al-Zaher came and, with an admiring glance, started counting the fish. There was one *musht athathi*, three *qishri* fish, still young, four *karseen*, four *marmour*, two big *balbout* and five or six black *athathi*.

Every sort of fish. What a fine, tasty meal they'd have this lunchtime! His aunt was still lost in thought, staring at some point in the heart of the lake, beyond the fishing boats. Maybe she was thinking of some spring past, full of tranquillity, comfort and goodness, and of a spring approaching when there'd be no peace of mind, when only God knew what would happen.

What memories it woke, this tent she'd made herself from goat hair over the past three seasons. One spring, in the shearing season there at the Duwair estate, she'd gathered an enormous mass of black goat hair. The herdsmen, all singing together, had washed it in the Yarmouk river, then they'd spread it out on stones on a blazingly hot day—the hot season came early in these lowlands. When it was dry, she'd cleaned it with a special comb, taking out any nettles and dirt, then, with her own hands, she'd turned it into balls, which she'd spun into thread with a spindle.

Radi remembered how, in those days, his aunt, the "sister of men" as people called her, would get started early in the morning, at first light, weaving on and on, joining night and day.

She wouldn't let anyone help her. She'd measure the length with her arm, and judge the size just by looking, because a peasant's eye is as true as a proper measure.

Within a month she'd finished weaving the tent, each piece separately.Then she'd bound the pieces together and the shepherds had come to prepare the poles and pegs and ropes. They'd worked vigorously, singing all together, and within hours the tent was standing tall atop the Duwair hill. And afterwards the "sister of men" sat with them in the afternoon, making coffee for them in place of Haj Hussein. Her husband was there, it was true, but she was the one who gave the orders. The husband was slightly built, with a quiet, weak character, rarely saying a word in conversation. He never reacted to anything that went on—the only thing that drew him out of his silence was the voice of his wife, for whom he had the greatest respect.

"This really is a big *balbout*!" Khaled al-Zaher said, staring at the fish which, its gills flared, was still leaping about as though clinging to life.

The aunt raised her hand and wiped the corners of her eyes, as if to wipe away a tear. What was it that made her so sad this particular noonday?

"Put that fish back in the water," she said.

She gestured to the still moving fish, and added:

"It's getting on my nerves."

The fish had its mouth wide open now, as though imploring help.

Radi bent down and picked up the flapping fish, which almost slipped through his hands. Then, to the amazement of the onlookers, he flung it back in the water.

When she'd finished washing the utensils, Badriyyeh came up to him.

"What did you do that for?" she asked.

He didn't answer. His aunt took a few steps, then turned and said:

"I'm off now. Come home when the tent's dried."

She took a few more steps, walking as if to chase away black thoughts. She stopped, threw a quick glance back, then went on.

"I think I understand," Radi said to himself.

"Just a moment, aunt," Khaled al-Zaher called out. "I'll harness the horse to the cart."

This time she didn't turn around.

"I want to walk on my two legs," she said impatiently. Then, holding her tall body erect, she went on and climbed the stone steps.

The children started jumping around again, making a lot of noise.

In the afternoon the waters of the lake turned turbid. The children went off, back to where they'd come from. Khaled al-Zaher put the pieces of tent in the cart, where the horse, already fed and watered, stood ready to go. As he jumped in and took the reins in his hands, Radi leaped in beside him, then put the fish trap between his legs. From above the shoreline Radi looked at the waters with their changing colors.

"I wonder what made your aunt act like that?" said Khaled al-Zaher.

Before Radi could reply, the roar of the glider reached them, getting higher as the plane moved away from the barrels.

Radi gazed at it intently as it sped over the surface of the lake, made murky now by the winds, the high waves and the sand. Still speeding on its gliders, it started to take off, in a wide arc on the horizon. Then it rose high and sped away, becoming a mere dot and, finally, vanishing behind some stray clouds in the open expanse of the sky.

The horse trotted powerfully along, despite the heavy load. Khaled al-Zaher was lost in his thoughts, and Radi, who was starting to think more about things, wondered in his turn: "What made my aunt so sad? Why did she act like that?"

Chapter Three

From the account of Abd al-Rahman the Iraqi

I emerged from the furnace of the desert. From between the grains of sand. The winds surrendered me to the winds, and the frost nipped my nose and the tips of my fingers.

I'd ridden in a hired car from Baghdad to the al-Habbaniyyeh crossroads. Then, for countless numbers of hours, I'd walked. No luggage and no passport. Still I'd walked, avoiding the police patrols. I was thirsty. The desert, heavy with the iciness of January, spat me out. How bitter the desert cold is! How often I remembered the midday sun, the summer heat and the sun-baked ground. How often I adjured the sun to unleash its arrows and burn my face with its scorching heat.

The cold of the desert, at that time of year, was crueller than the whips of Nouri al-Said's police. What a fearful night I spent, out there in the open, wretchedly huddled in a ditch by the side of the road. And how terrified I was when I heard that howling from the heart of the desert—from a wounded wolf, maybe, or a hungry hyena.

It was a cold night, with the taste of bitter tears. I slept on the spiky frost till a truck carrying sheep picked me up at dawn. When I heard the sound of its engines I climbed out of my ditch, desperate to preserve my life, and threw myself in front of it. The driver hesitated, then stepped on the brakes. Perhaps he realized where I was going: there were a lot of men crossing the desert these days, on their way to Palestine.

When the truck stopped, I ran up to it, bruised and torn. I don't recall what the driver asked me, or what I answered, but with my last strength I climbed in the back and fell asleep among the frightened, restless sheep. I slept over the droppings but beneath the warm wool. I slept on an empty stomach, utterly worn out for all my hunger, wrapped in the breath of these animals.

I only woke when the truck came to a stop, and the driver peered through the window and called out:

"We're at Duma. Sorry, but you'll have to get out."

I gathered my breath, got to my feet and, with what strength I had left, jumped down. I felt the hardness of the ground through my extreme faintness. The truck left, and I threw a glance at those feeble creatures being driven off to the slaughterhouse. Soon they'd be slaughtered and flayed, and then they'd be hung from hooks. I gazed at them as they disappeared behind a trail of dust, hardly able to keep my eyes open in the morning glare.

I found myself standing near the main town square, which, for all the bitter cold, was crowded with people all wearing headdresses, rolling cigarettes and crowding around the vendors.

How delicious it was, the smell of falafel being fried on a cold day!

I put my hand in my pocket and fingered the ten dinar note, but the vendor, a native of the town, his head wrapped up in the Damascene headdress, handed me the food and insisted he wouldn't take a penny. After filling my stomach I started exploring the town.

Here I was in al-Guta. I'd left the desert behind me. I'd left al-Rutba, and Abu al-Shamat and the howling of mangy wolves—and I'd left Baghdad, and the rushing waters of the Tigris that still flowed in its endless course, with no one knowing of the pains that gnawed its depths when night fell, and the men of Nouri al-Said and Abd al-Ilah started prowling the alleys and listening in at windows.

Oh, Abd al-Rahman bin Kazim, how utterly tired I am of all those discussions, going on all year long, between the intellectuals, the gentlemen and the educated people in the cafés of al-Rashid street, and between the two underground parties with their burning support for the nationalist struggle. Newspapers, broadcasts, debates—newspaper talk. Night talk wiped out by the day. Could anything possibly mean more than what I've done?

I walked through al-Guta, on to Damascus, reaching it from Bab Tuma and passing through the Amara district; then, walking from street to street, I found myself in Marjeh Square. O glorious face of Damascus! Now I had to find the place where I could see al-Kawuqji. I was carrying a piece of paper with a message to him from my uncle, al-Hajji, who'd served with him in the 1936 revolt.

My uncle, though, was no longer the man he'd been. Old age had come on him and sickness had made its home in his body. When he read my thoughts that evening, as we sat eating together, he poured the sauce over the rice, threw me a sharp glance, then said:

"So be it. It's God's will. God has inspired you, and you're responding to the call to war. Go off, then, and I'll give you a recommendation to al-Kawuqji."

I went to the general headquarters in Qudsiyyeh and had no difficulty meeting al-Kawuqji. In fact I found myself in front of him quicker than I'd expected. As I entered his presence, I felt nervous, with a sense of secret awe, for this was the man whose name was on everyone's lips.

He was wearing a yellow headdress held in place by a band,

and his face had a lean look, quite different from the sketches of him in the newspapers. He looked up from the piece of paper, which the orderly had taken in to him, then glanced at me piercingly.

"So how is your uncle?" he asked.

He said the words with no great enthusiasm, more, it seemed, by way of civility.

"You want to volunteer," he went on. "Right. You're a school teacher, a man of education. That's good."

He nodded, and inspected my dirty clothes without disapproval; it was as though he realized I'd crossed the desert on foot. Then he rang a bell and one of his assistants came in. He ordered that I be referred to the General Inspectorate to have my name registered, and be given a small sum to buy new clothes and to go to the public baths. I stayed one night at the Mashraq Hotel, in Marjeh Square, where I washed and had a shave. I'd bought some new clothes, and I slept the way I hadn't slept since the idea of volunteering first started to obsess me. Next morning I met the man who became one of my dearest friends. His name was Asad al-Shahba, and I met him at breakfast. The restaurant was crowded, and the only vacant seat was at his table.

I asked if I could sit down, and he said I could. The table was white marble. My friend had ordered a plate of beans with a loaf of hot *tannour** bread.

"Please join me," he said.

He spoke with a generosity that was clearly sincere—you could see it in his cheerful face—and I took a bite of the bread without any embarrassment. So it was I broke bread with him for the first time.

Asad al-Shahba—may his brave heart be filled with peace—

* *Tannour*: An open oven, with domed walls on which rounded loaves are placed for baking.

leaped to his feet when he learned I'd come to volunteer for the Liberation Army.

"If you're eager to start," he said, "come to the Qatanna camp with me."

He'd just, he said, finished his own military training. He sat down again, then said, gently and compassionately:

"Don't be too shocked by the sort of state we're in. Our army needs qualified instructors, and clothes and weapons and ammunition. We're only just starting out," he added. "The commander's promised we'll have everything we need in time."

I was hardly going to hesitate. I'd braced myself to put up with any hardship to reach the soil of Palestine.

Suddenly a waiter appeared and, bending down, whispered something in Asad al-Shahba's ear and gestured toward the entrance. A woman was standing there in the doorway, wrapped in the Damascene cloak, her face covered with a fine black veil. Only the palms of her hands, colored with henna, were visible. He turned pale and his manner grew confused. He got up and went over to her, taking her with him to a corner of the hotel.

He was away for some time, then he returned with a show of nonchalance and tried to take up the thread of our conversation where we'd left it; but I couldn't help noticing—though I refrained from remarking on it—that his right hand was shaking and that, though he was talking once more of the camp at Qatanna, he seemed confused as he drank his cold glass of tea. After a while he got control of himself and stood up.

"Come on," he said. "Get your stuff and we'll leave."

I went with him from Damascus to Qatanna. Waiting for him in Marjeh Square was a military vehicle carrying provisions, which was why the seats, roof, front window, and even the driver's eyelashes it seemed, were covered in flour.

On the way he talked about his home town of Aleppo, and about his family, and Qatanna, and training, and about the chaos and the long waiting. He told me about the Parachute rifle and the Brown cannon, about the Bazooka that needed repairing, the Vickers cannons with no ammunition, and the Browning cannon that needed to be transported, only they couldn't find an armored half-track.

"You'll have to be patient," he said. "Enthusiasm isn't enough on its own. If you're eager, and idealistic, you'll be shocked at the way things are. Don't be too depressed, our army's just getting started. For the first few days you'll think of going back where you came from. But don't do it. The call to war is more important than your expectations. Besides, what would you say to people?

"Learn from my experience. I was worried sick when I thought of going home. How could I go back? The young men from our neighborhood had come to Maarrat al-Numan to see me off. They'd fired shots in the air as a salute to gallantry and manhood, they'd sung songs celebrating courage, they'd stamped their feet in a *dabkeh** dance, in anticipation of the fire that would be lit on the mountain tops. In God's name, how could I leave the camp and go back to them with my head hanging?"

After that, nothing could demoralize me, not the chaos, or the conflicting orders of the officers, or the odd assortment of French and British and German weaponry. I did some training at Qatanna, then I was transferred to the Damir camp, where all was confusion and problems no one could find a solution to. I got used to hardships, to the insults of the instructors and the long list of grievances. I got used to waiting and the need for patience, as I adjusted to reality and to a cold that pierced the bones.

One night al-Kawuqji came in person. There was a good deal of

---

Dabkeh: Traditional folk dance of the Palestine countryside, also found in Syria and Lebanon.

noise and bustle beforehand, and someone came to alert us that the Commander was on his way. Suddenly the fearsome instructor was transformed into a gentle lamb. He addressed us warmly, urging us not to let him down in front of the Commander.

When the Commander's car arrived we were standing in a column waiting for him. He got out, wrapped up in a heavy winter coat and carrying his cane, followed by other officers whose elegance was stamped all over their faces and clothes. The camp commander approached him and saluted, while at the back the instructor had already given the signal, and we stiffly stood at attention.

Al-Kawuqji inspected the column, looking at some of the faces in the front row. Next he looked over our assortment of clothes, and our shoes, no two pairs of them alike. Then he shook his head. Was it a gesture of pained regret?

He motioned to the instructor, who signalled us to stand at ease. Then the Commander spoke a few words, to the effect that it was now time to start our work. At least it wasn't a long talk. Had he noticed how thin our clothes were as we shivered in this camp huddled at the gates of the desert? Finally, he walked off into the commanding officer's tent, followed by his officers.

The next day trucks came to take us back to Qatanna. In the crush I met up with Asad al-Shahba, who'd come eagerly looking for me, and I felt as though I'd been reunited with a childhood friend. He told me what he'd learned: that we were due to be transferred from Qatanna to our appointed positions in Palestine.

What a glorious moment that was! My heart pounded violently, and I was swept by dread followed by a sense of joy. They started issuing us thick winter clothing, military helmets, rifles, and cartridge pouches with a hundred shots. I realized then that we were heading for the battlefield.

×

The motorized convoy moved off before daybreak. I was sitting in the back of a carrier, and there were transport trucks in front of us and behind us. Chunks of mist showed through the pale yellow lights. Soon the darkness was ebbing as dawn approached.

There were several soldiers sitting alongside me, all young, all swathed in thick coats, carrying rifles of different makes. They were silent, overwhelmed by the awe of this long-awaited moment, thinking of military engagements, clashes, fire, of a flaming horizon and a bloody dawn and a fluttering banner.

After about an hour the deep silence started to be broken. One of them sang, in a tuneful voice:

"We must leave now. Farewell, my country."

Another young man took it up, then everyone started singing together, and I found myself joining them. In a few moments the barriers separating people were down, and just a few minutes after that the glow of friendship and familiarity had begun to spread. The warmth spread from throats to hands, and dawn gradually took on a milky white hue.

On the way to Deraa, people were waving to us from behind their plows and from the rooftops. Young women—Hourani peasant girls—were ululating at the top of their voices. We halted in the countryside to have our breakfast and relieve ourselves, and then on we went. The convoy stopped at a thicket on the outskirts of Deraa, to await further instructions.

Our company was the vanguard of the battalion, and there at the thicket we were introduced to our company commander, Ahmad Bey. Why he chose a name like that, and where the title of Bey came from, heaven only knows! He inspected the different groups and drank tea with us, talking a lot about the Jews and saying they were bastards. He never smiled once through the whole day.

We were there for a long time, waiting for our instructions. On the third day we learned from Ahmad Bey that negotiations were going on between the leader of the battalion, Lieutenant-Colonel Muhammad al-Safa, and the governor of Irbid Province, in the northeast of Jordan, about our passage through Jordan into Palestine. Glubb Pasha, so Ahmad Bey said, was stopping us from crossing, and some patriotic Jordanian officers were trying to manage something behind the scenes.

The issue was finally resolved on the fourth day, a day of overcast skies with black clouds, though with some blue showing between them. And so the convoy was on the move again. We passed through Deraa, then on through Ramtha. After that the road turned toward Irbid, then passed through Wadi al-Arab, Kufr Asad, the Wastiyyeh villages, Deir Abu Said and the northern Shuna Triangle. Finally we came to a halt near the tomb of the Prophet's Companion, Muadh ben Jabal.

It was a humble shrine, sought out by the poor who regarded it as blessed: they'd light candles in front of it and tie green ribbons to its windows. An aged sheikh looked after it. We spread out in the shade of this Companion, who'd come from the Arabian Peninsula to chase out the Roum from Palestine.

The site of the great Yarmouk battle wasn't too far off, Ahmad Bey told us—wrapping himself in his coat as he said it, and turning up his collar, though actually the cold wasn't as bitter here in this quiet part of the Jordan Rift. Through the drizzle I gazed at the mountains opposite, the mountains of Palestine. Only the river separated us from those dunes and plains, and it was just a short dash, so Ahmad Bey said, to our appointed position.

The next night the second company joined us, camping nearby, and the men from the two mixed together. And there among them was Asad al-Shahba, with his oversized coat, and his helmet and rifle, and his boisterous gaiety.

He gave me cigarettes, a tin of meat and an orange. "We'll soon be off toward the Damia bridge," he whispered. "It joins the two banks of the river. Then we'll cross over, to the site they've fixed for us in the Beisan valley."

How did he know all that?

We got ready to cross in small groups, and, while we were waiting, I sat and jotted down a few notes in my pad. Asad al-Shahba came up.

"What are you writing?" he asked.

"A letter to some friends," I replied evasively.

He pondered for a while, then said, diffidently:

"I might just need your beautiful words to write me a letter—"

Was he embarrassed, or had he just stumbled over the words?

The image of that woman wrapped in the Damascene cloak sprang to my mind, the woman who'd come to see him that morning, whose palms were covered with henna. I realized what it was he wanted and didn't need telling what I'd have to write.

He fell silent and took on a reserved air, maybe feeling he'd been too hasty, or else overcome by emotion. He flushed, his face taking on the same deep red color as the dye that covered her palms.

Just then a soldier from our company came up. The First Yarmouk Battalion, he told us joyfully, under the command of al-Shishikli, had attacked the settlement of Gadeen, near Tarshiha, to cover our crossing.

✖

The battalion broke up into small groups. Then we moved through the darkness toward the Damia bridge.

The transport trucks, cannons and supply cars crossed first, followed by the infantry of the second company. It was already dawn before my turn came, and we had to stay where we were until further notice, so as not to be seen. The rest of the companies were told to wait in a lemon grove on the banks of the Sharia river.

We watched the convoy that had crossed, as it moved off into the distance, envying our comrades who'd already set foot on the soil of Palestine.

The river was foaming and frothing from the heavy rains that had raised its level this year. It was like a sea, with waves crashing one against the other. No one, however strong, could have swum across to the other bank; it would have been madness even to think of it. Even boats, big or small, would have been swept away and capsized by the current. There was nothing for it but to wait for further orders.

The platoon still to cross was made up of three companies, and it wouldn't take us more than an hour to get over with our weaponry. No matter how long we had to wait, the night when we'd cross the Damia bridge to the west would come eventually.

Commander Muhammad al-Safa contacted us early next morning from his headquarters on the other bank. The soldier from the signal corps had been waiting impatiently for the message. I imagined Asad al-Shahba, his eyes full of tears from love for the soil of Palestine, and I felt my own heart pounding constantly, like a fist. No matter how long it took, we felt, we were bound to cross over to the other bank.

It didn't happen, though. A British force arrived, encircled the adjacent area and started dismantling the bridge. The order came to be on the alert.

"This is Glubb Pasha's doing," one of our comrades said.

No one came near us. The British troops were content to dismantle the bridge, taking the wood and iron off in their trucks and going back to where they'd come from.

That evening it rained heavily. The water swelled and surged blindly, almost bursting its banks. With the bridge dismantled, there was nothing connecting us to the other bank. We were on one side and our comrades were on the other, with just the wireless to keep us in touch. That evening an officer came from Damascus to assure us all would be well. Then, at midnight, he went back with some officers of the East Jordan army.

We were, it was decided, to hide in the backs of trucks carrying supplies to the Arab army corps in Jericho, across the Allenby Bridge. This had been arranged with some of the patriotic officers, who were furious with Glubb Pasha.

The trucks came at one in the morning, and in we climbed. Along with some others I got into the first one, which was carrying meat and vegetables. The meat was kept in open crates, and these gave out the smell of sheep who had grazed long in rich pastures, though they'd actually already been skinned. As the truck carried us side by side with these slaughtered sheep, I recalled the gentle creatures among whose wool I'd warmed myself on my trip from the Abu Shaamat desert to Duma, and I prayed from the bottom of my heart we wouldn't share their fate. The truck traveled on south along a narrow, deserted road, and within the hour we'd reached the Allenby Bridge, which was guarded by British troops.

I huddled into myself, imagining they'd discover us and stop us crossing. Everything, though, went quickly, with no problems. The soldier opened the barrier, and the trucks, their blazing headlights lighting up the palm trees on the other bank, crossed over.

It was all done in a few minutes. The trucks pressed on through the cold morning, stopping, eventually, on the outskirts of Jericho, where vehicles from the Arab Liberation Army were waiting for us. I transferred from one vehicle to the other, cold, hungry and dazed. I no longer knew what was going on. Between sleep and waking, I found the cars had came to a final stop at our new encampment.

Only then did it come home to me: I was treading the soil of Palestine.

✖

What surging enthusiasm, what heady dreams they had, those men from Syria and Iraq and Egypt! And how brave they were!

Discord and petty disagreement melted away, and they all beat as if with one heart. The companies were dissolved and reorganized. I was in the same company as Asad al-Shahba now, and we started spending most of our time together, cleaning rifles, maintaining the guns, discussing news, and, through the long nights, talking together, each giving the other an account of his life and the problems he'd had to face.

Whenever the subject turned to women, Asad al-Shahba's face would darken, and then I'd remember that tall woman, her body wrapped in a Damascene cloak, hiding God knows what bright face behind the delicate black veil.

One day, while I was writing my account in my small notebook, he came up to me.

"It's time," he said abruptly, "I told you about me and that woman. Do you remember her?"

I smiled at him as he squatted there opposite me outside the tent, positively beaming with joy. What impulse had driven him to tell me the story?

He told it with the yearning of a soldier tormented by memories, swept away by his imagination. He was in the grip of emotion, to the tips of his trembling fingers.

"When I left Aleppo," he said, "and went on to Damascus, I had to wait a few days before I could join the camp at Qatanna."

He looked at me as he said it, to be sure I was interested in the story he had to tell. I laid my notebook and pen aside to show I was, and he relaxed and went on.

"The three days I was supposed to wait there turned into three weeks, and during that time I stayed at my uncle's house in the Amara district. My uncle's a thoroughly good, loyal man; he has the common touch, but he's a gentleman too. He prays, he fasts, he reads the Quran, but at the same time he likes his pleasures: late nights, singing, entertainment and enjoyment. He plays the *oud*[*], and his food and clothes and furniture are all elegant. He likes to drink his morning coffee at the fountain in the center of the house, while his Damascene wife waters the blooming flower beds.

"My uncle and his wife have lived alone since their only daughter married, and, though they're both getting older now, they're devoted to one another, the way birds are. He dresses her in the finest clothes and fills her arms with bracelets, and she gives him purity and cleanliness and peace of mind.

"When I knocked on their door, they gave me a marvelous, overwhelming welcome. My being there added liveliness to their house, which was fragrant with the scent of jasmine. During the day I'd go with my uncle to his cloth shop in the Hamidiyyeh Souk, where, in front of the other merchants, he'd show how proud he was of the patriotism of his nephew, who was on his way from Aleppo to Palestine.

"After a few days I was well known in the neighborhood, and my uncle even took me to Sheikh Muhammad al-Ashmar's council at Bab al-Musalli. Every day I'd go to Qudsiyyeh to check with the General Inspectorate, burning with eagerness to join the camp at Qatanna. But they always told me to wait.

"It was during all this that I met a young lady named Malak. I saw her first as I was passing through the alley to my uncle's house. She was standing watering the jasmine that climbed up her window, and she didn't draw back when she saw me, or close the curtains. God, what a beauty it was that lit up my soul—and what a tremor took hold of my heart!

"Our eyes met. Was there a hint of a smile on her lips?

---

* *Oud*: Pear-shaped, short necked, fretless instrument with five double courses of nylon or gut and metal-wound silk strings.

"It all happened in a few seconds, as I went up to my uncle's house, then slowed down, stood at the door, knocked and went in, the pounding of my heart nearly giving me away.

"'You look pale,' my uncle's wife said. 'Are you tired?' I hid my confusion behind a smile and went off to my room.

"Next day I left the house early, before my uncle, and walked slowly with my eyes on her window. The curtains were drawn, but when I passed in front of the window I sensed the curtain fluttered, as though someone was there watching me.

"I spent the day walking about aimlessly, on and on. I went through the Marjeh district to the Seven Fountains, then on to the Sheikh Mihye al-Din district. I needed to be quiet and on my own. I needed to fill my lungs with fresh air, with the cool breeze that brings tears to the eyes.

"I went back in the evening, passing though the alley step by deliberate step. The window was shut tight. There was no ray of hope.

"I knocked at the door, and my uncle greeted me with a storm of protest.

"'Where have you been?' he said. 'We've been looking for you everywhere. We were waiting for you to have lunch with us.'

"'We were afraid something had happened to you,' my uncle's wife said.

"I did my best to act normally, but I couldn't help looking despondent. My uncle, maybe sensing I was tired out, respected my wish for quiet, letting me go to bed early, not expecting me to keep him company through one of his long nights.

"Next morning I opened the front door—and there she was, standing at the entrance to her house, as though we had an appointment! When she saw me, she let down her veil. She was wrapped in a black cloak, her body tall and slim. She walked ahead of me in high-heeled shoes, and I caught a glimpse of the henna on the palms of her hands.

"I followed her. There were only children in the alley. I walked on till I came alongside her, my heart pounding. I wanted to say something to her, but lost my nerve at the last moment. She walked on without turning around, finally coming to a stop at the tram station. There were a number of people waiting, so I stood there among them; and when the tram arrived, and they got on, so did I.

"I found myself opposite her—face to face. She was looking at me through her thin veil, and I felt her glances falling like oil over the fire that was raging in my heart.

"The tram came to a halt at Marjeh Square. She got off, and I followed her. She walked this way and that, and I stayed behind her, though careful to leave a safe distance between us, so as not to arouse people's suspicions. She walked beside the river Barada, aimlessly it seemed, because then she turned toward the Hijaz station and stood in front of some shop windows looking at the dresses and scent. Could she see me reflected in the windows, as I stood and watched her on the pavement opposite?

"She crossed the street, passing in front of the post office, then the broadcasting station, then the Palace of Justice, and finally walking toward the fire station. Once she turned around, and I thought she was going to stop and say something to me. Then she moved on again like a breeze.

"My courage had failed me. I didn't know what to do.

"She went into a shop that sold threads and buttons and general haberdashery. There she partly lifted her veil as she looked the buttons over, bought what she wanted, then left the shop like some mettlesome doe.

"She went on to the souk, and I almost lost her in the crowd there. But though there were a lot of women in black cloaks, moving in all directions, I always knew which one was her.

"She went into the silk market, where the narrow alleys displayed cloth of every color and sort, and the smell of incense spread through the openings and arcades. She stopped at a shop and had the shopkeeper bring down different materials to spread in front of her, then bought a few meters of red gossamer silk.

"After that she went on to the perfume market. What piercing scents there were; and there were women and young girls—and vendors well used to dealing with them, vendors who addressed the women with honeyed words, daring and rather vulgar. They spoke to her in a way that was pretty well flirtatious, but she took no notice. Was she maybe trying to work up my jealousy?

"I tell you, frankly, I did feel jealousy gnawing away at me, fraying my nerves. I only relaxed when she left the perfume market. Where was she going now?

"She went by me without so much as a glance, though, just as she passed, she let her cloak slip off her shoulder, and I glimpsed her dress, printed with lilac flowers, before she pulled the cloak up again. She went back into the crowded street, and once more I followed her, still unable to pluck up the courage to say anything.

"Now, once again, she was standing at the tram station, where some school children were waiting too. I sidled up to within an arm's length of her. I could smell the scent of flowers wafting out from beneath her cloak.

"Now! My heart beat louder, the sweat poured from my forehead. Should I speak to her? I was too nervous—I didn't dare.

"Several moments passed, full of an unfamiliar anxiety. Then the tram arrived. The school children got on, and so did we.

"I sat on a seat facing her. I could make out her features behind the thin veil hiding her face. We got off at the last stop, and by then I'd prepared myself to speak to her. I was determined, now, not to miss this chance. The street, though, was crowded with people, and I was forced to leave a distance between us.

"In the alley leading to the house there was an old woman from the neighborhood, walking halfway between us, and so the chance was lost. But when she went into her house, she left the door ajar and, lifting her veil, pierced me with a look and a smile.

Then she closed the door."

Asad al-Shahba fell silent. His face, it seemed to me, was radiant with light. What feelings were swelling inside him, here among these great plains? He said no more. I waited for him to go on, but Saber, the young man who sang with a voice of pure gold, came and interrupted us.

That evening Asad al-Shahba was silent as never before; and when he'd gone off to his tent and I'd gone to bed, I tried to guess what had happened next, what secret lay concealed behind that woman with the henna palms, what force had drawn her tender heart toward his that was more tender still.

I tried to finish off the story, to imagine what had happened after she pierced him with that look from her eyes, then closed the door. I strove, vainly, to catch the meaning behind that elaborate rhapsody of his. It was all to no avail.

The following days were completely taken up with training and reconnaissance, and with live ammunition maneuvers. Enthusiasm reached a fever pitch. We would, our commander told us, be operating in the region between Beisan and Jenin.

We learned, too, that further forces were due to join us, and that al-Kawuqji was transferring his headquarters from Qudsiyyeh to Tulkarm. Our company commander, Ahmad Bey, was busily visiting people in the surrounding areas, and we were, we felt, on the verge of starting operations.

This belief was reinforced by the arrival of the Circassian troops, though Asad al-Shahba, who had a talent for flushing out bits of special news, whispered they were really there to bolster Ahmad Bey's standing, since he'd found most people supported the Mufti and the forces the latter was beginning to mobilize.

We were longing to join the fighting, and our chance came at last when we were assigned to defend a reconnaissance unit charged with collecting intelligence about the settlement of Tirat-Zevi, which the local people called al-Ziraa. We had, though, no direct fighting with the enemy, since our men were disguised as peasants and remained undiscovered.

After this successful operation, Ahmad Bey allowed us one day's leave. And what in the name of God were we to do with a day's leave in these great, open plains? We weren't allowed to wander about in the villages, so what leave actually meant was that you could stay asleep in your tent without anyone waking you up, or be lazy any way you wanted, or wash your socks and underclothes when you felt like it.

We slept in, then, after breakfast, we walked about, or ran, and gathered a few edible wild plants like fennel, *akkoub, marar* and vetch. Then we sat together smoking and looking forward to the days ahead.

We talked about all sorts of things. We discussed the conflict between the Mufti and al-Kawuqji, we talked of the meetings of the Arab League, then moved on to our small adventures with women. I tried to get Asad al-Shahba to talk about that woman with the henna palms, without actually mentioning her. "So what happened finally?" I asked. He gave a rather hesitant smile, but I prodded him on to finish the story. He was silent for a few moments, as though dredging things up from deep inside. Then he began.

"Three days passed," he said, "and I couldn't get to see her. Her door was closed, and so was the window, although the jasmine hanging from it looked green and healthy. I did, though, manage to outwit my uncle's wife and get some information about the people in the house. They were from the Hadou family. The father had a leather shop in al-Suweika, while her mother was a professional dressmaker, whose customers were mostly al-Guta peasants. The girl's name was Malak, and she was the eldest child, but she had two brothers, one of them retarded.

"Malak helped her mother, and she was actually the one who went to the market to buy the threads and buttons and other things necessary. That was why her trips to the market didn't attract any attention; and perhaps that's what made her bold and so brimming with initiative. Three days passed, as I said, and still I didn't see her. Had my uncle's wife, I wondered, noticed what was happening? Had she made the connection between my anxiety and my endless questions about the people in that house?

"My uncle's wife was a good woman, and she had enough common sense, too, to see what was going on. One sunny morning, after we'd drunk our coffee together, she said: 'Turn your cup over, so I can read your fortune.'

"She stared into the cup. 'All the paths in your cup are open,' she said, 'and that's a good sign. I can see a big window there too. That means relief after a time of hardship.'

"There was a brief silence. Then she turned the cup over twice, and added:

"'There's the key, look!'

"I looked, but couldn't make anything of the crisscross patterns the coffee dregs had left. She winked at my uncle.

"'The key's a silver one,' she said. 'What it needs is a door, and the door needs a wall, and the wall needs a roof. The roof's a kind of shield, and the shield means a good woman, and a good woman can be found. Look in your heart and you'll find her.'

My uncle laughed and clapped his hands.

"'Woman,' he said, 'you've got just one thing on your mind, while everyone else in the world's thinking of other things. My nephew's volunteered to go to war. Tell him something about that road.'

"I realized then my uncle's wife had kept my secret, and I was actually delighted by what she'd said.

"As I left the house with my uncle, the window was still shut. I rode with him in the cart that waited for him, every morning,

at the top of the street, reflecting on my uncle's wife who'd found out my secret.

"Then, as the cart set off, I saw her, wrapped in her cloak with a light stick in her hand. I could have recognized her among a thousand women! My uncle went on talking, but I wasn't hearing what he said. As the cart overtook her, I felt my heart sink into my boots.

"Had she seen me? Had she deigned to cast a glance at this cart, pulled along by an ancient horse that was spurred on by a driver more ancient still? I couldn't do a thing. I couldn't, for instance, tell my uncle I wanted to get off. Anything I did would surely give me away. And just what would my uncle have to say about his nephew, the fighter, amusing himself by chasing girls?

"All the way I did my utmost to think of nothing but the war. Giving free rein to this frivolous heart of mine would, I felt, only distract me from the goal to which I'd dedicated myself. God, I told myself, was testing my strength, testing my will and resolve. I must bear up and forget all about this girl. Finally I persuaded myself I should go to Qudsiyyeh and stay there till I was sent to the training camp.

"Accordingly, at the gates of the Hamidiyyeh souk, I told my uncle I wanted to get out. I was going off to Qudsiyyeh, I said. He gave me his blessing and wished me luck.

"I walked to Marjeh Square to try and find some transport. And there, in the midst of the bustle, I saw her! We met suddenly—face to face! It was a glorious coincidence.

"All the ideas I'd been piecing together collapsed, and I found myself going eagerly up to her. She stopped. This time, though, she didn't pass on again like the breeze, but stood there, a heady scent coming from her.

"'Hello,' I said.

"'Welcome,' she answered, from behind her transparent black veil.

"I trembled from the top of my head to the tips of my fingers. She walked, and I walked alongside her. We were near a fountain, and the spray fell on us.

"'So,' she said, as though we were old acquaintances, 'you've volunteered for the war in Palestine.'

"Did she admire me for it, or was she disapproving?

"'The Jews are moving forward like locusts,' I answered. 'Eating everything, green or dry.'

"That was how it started. That's how we got to know one another.

"She didn't say what she thought of my plans. She did say, though, the talk about me in the neighborhood had aroused her interest.

"'Where are you going?' I asked.

"She hesitated for a moment, then said: 'To al-Muhajireen.'

"There was a secret complicity between us now.

"'I'm going to al-Muhajireen too,' I said.

"We boarded the tram, the slow tram that ran by the river. It turned into al-Salhiyyeh, passing in front of the Parliament, then moved on to Arnous square, then to Jisr al-Abyad, where we reached our destination.

"At the last stop she lifted her veil, looked at me with her captivating eyes. and asked:

"'When will you be going to the front?'

"There were passengers getting off and others boarding. The conductor started collecting fares. We didn't think of getting off; the important thing was we were sitting there side by side.

"'I'm afraid for you,' her eyes said. Then she let down her veil and asked once more:

"'When will you be going to the front?'

"'Very soon, God willing,' I answered.

"At al-Salhiyyeh she asked me to get off, so she could go on alone to Marjeh Square.

"'We shouldn't be seen together,' she said.

"Before getting off, I asked: 'When shall I see you again?'

"She didn't turn around.

"'Let's leave it to chance,' she said."

Asad al-Shahba paused. I thought he was going to stop, the way he had before, but instead he looked at me and smiled.

"I'll tell you what happened next," he went on. "I left her to go on alone, while I went off to Qudsiyyeh. And what do you think? They were waiting for me! Within the hour I had my papers and I was on my way to Qatanna. I couldn't even tell my uncle, because they insisted I mustn't let any relatives know where I'd be. I went through three weeks of hard, intensive training.

"There was no time for memories, and my meeting with that girl came to seem like a mere passing whim. To tell the truth, the training was harsh enough to make you forget the milk you'd drunk at your mother's breast. After three weeks of it, I'd lost a good deal of weight.

"At the end of it they gave me a three-day leave, with some money for expenses. I didn't feel like going to Aleppo—what would people say, when they'd supposed I was already fighting on Palestinian soil? So I booked a room in a hotel, bought some clothes, washed and shaved, then put on my new clothes and raced off to my uncle's house.

"My uncle's wife opened the door, and seemed thoroughly taken aback. Maybe I looked different after training, especially as they'd cut my long hair. She raised her eyebrows.

"'What's happened to you, son?' she said.

"The moment we sat down she started saying how worried she was about the weight I'd lost and about how weak I looked. Then she served me some rose water. My uncle still wasn't back from his night out, but I was tired and, to tell the truth, anxious for news on one particular topic. I told my uncle's wife I'd like a cup of coffee.

"She went off to the kitchen, but came back quickly, as though she'd guessed why I wanted the coffee. She tried to fight back a smile, then said:

"'I won't read your fortune this time.'

"I laughed, and that encouraged her to draw me out.

"'You want to hear about our neighbors, don't you?' she said. 'Well, they've been asking after you a lot. Why don't you stop beating about the bush and tell me how things are?'

"This good woman, who was growing old now, was completely on my side. She had a very compassionate heart.

"'If you want her,' she said, 'then ask for her hand in marriage. Tie her to you with a ring and let things work themselves out afterwards. But be careful too, son. Gossip and rumors spread quickly in our neighborhood, and she's from a respectable family. If you're not really serious, then leave things alone.' She said that firmly enough, but still, from time to time, she'd make remarks about Malak's good points and the skills she had.

"At that point my uncle arrived. She said nothing more, and I knew, from her silence, that my uncle still had no inkling of what was happening. He was angry when he learned I'd booked a room at the hotel, and wouldn't calm down until I'd promised to come and stay at his home.

"We had one of our old evenings. I told him about the harsh training, and afterwards we played backgammon and I let him win. After that we had supper, then we all went to bed.

"Next morning my uncle went out early, while I was still asleep. In fact I was so exhausted I slept till noon. Then I woke, washed and had breakfast.

"'Why didn't you talk to your uncle about it?' she asked. 'Aren't you serious about things?'

"I felt then that the whole thing had lost its charm and sweetness. The secret was losing its mysterious attraction. If matters went the way my uncle's wife wanted them to, I'd lose all the pleasure

of my anxiety, the watching and waiting and confusion. Not knowing what to say to her, I took refuge in silence.

"Then I left her and went out. I don't know if she sensed, at that moment, how confused and lost I felt, or whether she'd started having doubts about my real intentions. At any rate, her eyes followed me as I crossed the inner courtyard toward the front door, and I caught some words that sounded very much like the good wishes my mother would have expressed for me.

"The alley was empty, and her door and window were both shut. At the top of the alley I plunged into the crowds. Then I went back to my hotel, where I met some of my comrades from the training camp. Most of the soldiers from the Liberation Army were staying there.

"We went off to al-Rabwa, and there, on the banks of the Barada, we ate grilled meat and fruit, and, through the gurgling of *nargilas*, talked of battle and medals and dust and flames. Finally we went back to our hotel, filled with our heady dreams.

"There at the hotel I found my uncle waiting for me, sitting on a chair with his *tarboush** alongside him and fingering his prayer beads. He jumped up when he saw me, put his *tarboush* back on, gripped his cane and said, with authority:

"'You're not getting away today. Come on.'

"Outside the cart was waiting. He pushed me on to it, then sat down alongside me. The cart started off slowly, but soon picked up speed.

"'I've been looking for you in all the Marjeh Square hotels,' he said. Then he added: 'I've been praying at the Umayyad Mosque too, asking God to give you victory.'

"When we reached his house he changed into a loose gown. A little later there was a knock at the door.

"'I forgot to tell you,' he said. 'There's a guest coming.'

---

* *Tarboush*: A fez.

"A man came in, a man in early middle age, slimly built, with handsome features and elegant clothes. My uncle introduced him to me as his neighbor Abu Qassem Hadou; and I realized then the lunch had been carefully planned, and that my uncle's wife was starting to go too far.

"The man was clearly pleased with his smart appearance. As my uncle was introducing him, he took off his *tarboush* and opened up part of his white jacket to show a gold watch hanging on a chain from his pocket.

"'This is my nephew,' my uncle said, 'the one I was telling you about. His father owns the biggest kebab restaurant in Aleppo and his mother's from a good, well-known family. He's going off to Palestine to fight, but he won't be there too long.'

"As the man sat down, he added:

"'The war isn't going to last long. Just a quick scramble to throw out those wretched Jews.'

"The man sat down, leaned back on a cushion and plunged straight into some news he'd heard on the Near East Radio, along with an account of the declaration made by President Shukri al-Quwwatli and others. Meanwhile my uncle's wife was preparing the food, and I went back to the kitchen, where there was a smell of cooking and a lot of steam, along with a noise from the stove that meant I had to raise my voice to talk to her. I was going to ask her what this sudden invitation of Malak's father was all about, and, on top of that, to tell her I wouldn't be needing any lunch, as I'd already eaten with my comrades. I was sure she'd told my uncle how things stood, and I found myself, as a result, pitched into a situation where I had no idea how to behave.

"When, though, she prepared the lunch table, laden with rice, meats and different kinds of stuffed vegetables and vine leaves, I didn't dare say I wasn't hungry. I forced the food down as my uncle and our guest discussed Ibrahim Hanano, and Sultan Pasha, and Sheikh Muhammad al-Ashmar, and the resistance at al-Guta, and the imminent independence. After lunch I tried to be the perfect host, pouring water over the guest's hands, then, following my aunt's directions from behind the curtain, serving coffee and fruit.

"After lunch my uncle played a game of backgammon with his guest, while I played my part by watching attentively. I could feel all the special emotions, which I'd harbored for so long, melting away. My only thought, all I wanted in the world, was to get back to the army camp.

"When the guest had left my uncle expressed his pleasure, and my uncle's wife, too, seemed thoroughly happy at the way things had gone. She started talking pleasantly to me, prodding me on to broach the subject, but I took no notice.

"'So nephew,' my uncle said playfully, 'soon you'll be off to war. We'll be thinking of you, waiting for you to come back. It mightn't be a bad idea to get you engaged to some nice girl, to remind you there's someone waiting for you.'

"His wife added all kinds of things, which only made me more embarrassed and confused and worried. I felt miserable they'd found out my secret and prepared a line of retreat. 'If I do come back safe and sound,' I said, 'I'll certainly think about it.'

"For all their insistence I left things in the air, and, that evening, made my way to the hotel and from there to the camp at Qatanna."

Asad al-Shahba paused once more, making me even more curious.

"What happened then?" I asked.

The sun was finally setting behind some light clouds.

"It's getting late," he said. "But I'll tell you quickly how it finished. It was a long time before I had another leave, and then I stayed at the hotel and went to visit my uncle at his shop, avoiding a visit to the house by telling him I only had an hour and would have to get straight back to my post. Then I spent the rest of the day at the Brazil Café.

"Next morning, if you remember, you and I met at breakfast, and Malak herself came along to ask about me. How did she know where I was? Who told her to go to that hotel? Was it my aunt's chattering tongue, or another one of her arrangements?

"I was taken aback to see her there, shaken to the core—and my amazement was mixed up with all those old familiar feelings, stirred up all over again. She was waiting for me at the door. I took hold of her hand and had her sit down in a corner of the hotel.

"'Why don't we see you any more?' she asked.

"She kept the veil over her face as she spoke, but a tremor in the voice betrayed a tear I couldn't see, not because of the veil but because I couldn't look into her face. She knew well enough I couldn't sit there with her long, because they don't like that sort of thing in these traditional hotels. After a short silence she took from her bosom a three-cornered amulet wrapped in a green cloth.

"'This amulet bears the words of God,' she said. 'It was written for me by Sheikh Azzam. I begged him to write an amulet, to protect you and bring you back safe.'

"Once again her voice trembled tearfully, and I felt an overwhelming desire to kiss her palms that were all henna-dyed. I found myself talking to her in a shaky voice, giving her my promise. Then I begged her to go back home.

"She walked away, turned once, then went on, and I turned back myself. All the birds, which I'd kept caged up in that sad heart of mine, took flight."

With these words Asad al-Shahba took from his pocket an amulet wrapped in green cloth. Then he fell into a silence I preferred not to break, leaving him to his own thoughts. We went on down the slope without another word.

At any rate Asad al-Shahba reported for duty next morning like a good soldier, carrying out his routine duties like weapon cleaning and helping in the kitchen. Every so often, though, he'd seek out some solitary spot where his thoughts could take flight, and he'd be as silent as a homing pigeon.

✖

Ahmad Bey didn't spend much time at the army camp now. He was moving around the villages, meeting the people, searching out new positions, trying to persuade the young men to join the Liberation Army. His task wasn't an easy one, because most people sympathized with the Mufti and the forces mobilized for the war by Abd al-Qader al-Husseini.

On the advice of the battalion commander, he was careful to go about without any attendants, or cars, or any signs of privilege that might put people off. And so he traveled in hired cars, slept in the houses of dignitaries, and occasionally braved it on foot for a fair distance. There was gossip he'd never walk at night because he was afraid of the pitch darkness then, but no one really believed it. It was surely inconceivable that Ahmad Bey, with all his power and dignity, should be weak and lacking in courage.

By mid-February the cold was bitter, and rain had started pouring. As the old stomach pains came back to plague me, I had to take to my bed. Adnan, the medical orderly, came around and gave me something to take, while Asad al-Shahba insisted on watching over me at night. Instead of sleeping after his turn of sentry duty, he'd come to my tent and sit up with me until morning.

Then, to add to my misfortunes, the battalion commander chose that moment to declare a state of alert. It was a stiff test of my strength, since I obviously couldn't stay and sleep while my comrades went off to battle. The first lieutenant, though, wouldn't let me join the assembly points, telling me, instead, to stay with the group assigned to guard the camp until Ahmad Bey returned.

He got back that very night—so I was told by Asad al-Shahba, who was one of those left on guard—and next morning Asad al-Shahba came to tell me Ahmad Bey had agreed I should take part. He handed me a whole belt of cartridges he'd somehow managed to lay his hands on, and promised to get me a Miles and a grenade before we set off.

That morning I was sitting at the entrance to my tent, writing my will, when a stranger in civilian clothes turned up suddenly, a young man of about twenty-five or perhaps a bit more. He stopped and greeted me.

As you might expect when a man's making his will, and writing emotional words to his mother, I didn't exactly welcome the intrusion. Still, he looked so lost I asked him, politely, to come and join me. He immediately squatted down beside me, his face showing confusion but innocence too.

"Are you new here?" I asked.

"I've just arrived," he replied.

He was, I realized then, a new volunteer from among the local people, who hadn't had his training yet and would no doubt soon be sent to Qatanna. I recalled my own worries and weariness, the hardships I'd faced as a new volunteer, and felt a wave of sympathy for this green, naive young man. I put my papers away.

It had started raining, and we went inside the tent. After he'd finished his guard duty Asad al-Shahba came in too, and we all spent the evening together. Little did I realize this new young man would become as dear a friend to me as Asad al-Shahba himself.

When I'd eventually finished my will, I put on my battle fatigues and hurried off to the assembly point, the forward position leading to the battle area itself.

✖

The attack on the Tirat-Zevi settlement began at three in the morning. The ground was soggy anyway from the rain, and when the settlers realized we were attacking they opened the hoses and drenched the surrounding areas with water, until they were like swamps.

The battle started, then, at three, and we opened fire with all the weapons we had; I was part of a supporting infantry company. The main assault force couldn't penetrate the settlement in the heavy rain. We targeted artillery fire on the towers to try to soften them up, but still the force couldn't advance.

By dawn the situation was hopeless. Reinforcements had reached Tirat-Zevi from nearby settlements and a counter-attack and bombardment had started. Our forces started to disperse, sinking in the mud, and our casualties were heavy. While I was helping the wounded here and there, a shell fell close to me and I was hit by shrapnel. I must have lost consciousness from the loss of blood, because I woke to find myself in the field hospital.

The night seemed to go on for ever, and I couldn't sleep. I felt as though I was lying on thorns. And no, it wasn't because of the wounds, still tender and green and scabless—that wasn't where the pain came from.

What a night it was, with everything finally silent, even the wind, and the frogs and dogs and hyenas and crickets. Only the pain screamed out from the depths of my soul. But it wasn't the wounds that left sleeplessness digging its claws down into my tortured spirit. It was the taste of those bitter moments that still washed over me, insistent and monotonous and sorrowful. I felt I had no strength left, that I was exhausted and finished. I felt dizzy, the very ground seemed to tremble, and my eyelids were heavy, though not with sleep. What a drawn-out ordeal that was!

Everything seemed wan and colorless, and despair slunk in to lurk behind the darkness and the lies, the chaos and the bungling. How bitter the taste of defeat is!

Pain, and grief, and sorrow. The field hospital. A doctor. An orderly. Cotton wool. Gauze. The smell of iodine. A thermometer. A shot into the vein. A shot into the muscle. Two pills three times before meals. Then defeat and the collapse of everything.

How had it happened? I could hardly believe it. Morale had been devastated, as that blow struck suddenly out of the blue.

Bombs and searchlights; water flooding and drowning the whole field. We'd had rain with us ever since we'd moved from al-Damir to Deraa the month before. We'd had it with us as we crossed the Damia Bridge, and it had followed us as all through the battle of al-Ziraa.

Water was pouring out and drenching the whole plain. The sky was pouring down. Water bubbled up out of the ground and tumbled down from the sky. What kind of hell was this? Unbearable pain. The wound was still fresh, but the taste of defeat was more unbearable still.

Asad al-Shahba came in with the medical orderly.

"Don't excite yourself, Abd al-Rahman," he said.

"I want to see Lieutenant-Colonel Muhammad al-Safa," I shouted at the medical orderly. "I want to see him now."

He felt my forehead to check my temperature.

"Don't excite yourself," Asad al-Shahba repeated, fighting back his tears now. He turned and went out, perhaps so as not to break down.

The orderly sat down. He may have realized what was firing the madness in my veins, but he didn't have the authority to get me to see the commander of the second Yarmouk battalion, with its three companies. I realized too, I think, that no one would dare tell Lieutenant-Colonel al-Safa of my demand. I suppose I just needed to scream out my pain. When the orderly came and told me to give him my arm for the injection, I didn't hesitate. I stretched it out and closed my eyes.

✖

I woke up to find everything calm. The rain had stopped, and the air was clear and filled with the pungent smell of earth. I can still see that thatched ceiling now. I can see the whitewashed wall. I can see the face of Adnan, the medical orderly, and the man in the next bed.

"Are you feeling all right now?" the orderly asked.

I felt my vision blurred, perhaps from the medicine. The patient in the next bed moaned deeply, a sound like something from the depths of a volcano, a moan of burning pain. Where had all this pain come from?

The orderly raised me up and put a pillow at my back. I could see now what was happening in the great room. The orderly was already standing by the next bed, standing and waiting. What was he waiting for? He was silent for a few moments, then said: "He was out there all night, lost in the open country. The frost got to him."

Lost in the open country? Was this one of the men who'd wandered about aimlessly, during that disastrous final stage of the battle? I gazed into his face – and found it was none other than the volunteer who'd just joined us, the young man Najib! He was unshaven, and his eyes were closed as though he was unconscious. Yet, every so often, he'd be racked by that terrible sigh, his adam's apple bobbing up and down.

Doesn't disaster seem easier to bear when you see another's? I recalled his smart-looking face, with its thin moustache, the way I'd seen him last when I was sick. He opened his eyes and realized he was in the hospital. Then, straight away, he spoke.

"The bullet-proof vest," he said. "Where's the vest? What have you done with it?"

They'd taken his clothes off him and wrapped him in blankets.

"Where's the bullet-proof vest?" he said again.

No one bothered to answer. The orderly just went off to read a newspaper.

For all my own pain and dizziness, I found myself answering, and, when he heard my voice, he opened his eyes. Perhaps he couldn't see clearly either, but he knew who I was.

"Aren't you Abd al-Rahman the Iraqi?" he groaned.

He stretched out his hand as though he wanted to feel my face, like a blind man sensing the presence of a son who'd been away.

"Aren't you Abd al-Rahman?" he repeated.

Were the tears his or mine? He was weeping quietly. Why was he weeping? What had led him to wander all night long, in the open fields? Why was there such utter bewilderment and loss marked on his face? Fighting back an urge to weep myself, I assumed an air of nonchalance.

"What's all this about a bullet-proof vest?" I said.

Either he didn't take the question in, or he pretended not to. He didn't answer, and he didn't mention the vest to me again until a month later, when I went to Damascus on leave and visited him at the camp in Qatanna—he'd been sent there by Ahmad Bey when he'd recovered. He'd been summoned to see Ahmad Bey, he said, and hadn't looked him in the eye but hadn't apologized either.

And so the matter had passed off, with neither making any reference to what had happened. Ahmad Bey had simply signed Najib's papers and sent him off for training.

There at the Qatanna camp everything changed: Najib became a different man, top of his group, the brightest fellow and the best shot. He became popular and well-loved in the camp, and even in the town of Qatanna itself and the surrounding district.

I persuaded the camp commander to give him a brief leave, and we went to Damascus together—to that same hotel in Marjeh Square. He wasn't sad-faced any more, and, like me, he'd forgotten

—or at any rate pretended to forget—what happened at Tirat-Zevi.

We didn't talk about those days. He just asked about the new positions we'd taken up between Jenin and Beisan, then went on to tell me about that wonderful bullet-proof vest a British soldier had sold to someone in Samakh, and how Ahmad Bey had bought it, then, later, told the Inspector-General's deputy it was part of the booty from the battle.

The Inspector-General's deputy knew well enough the battle had been lost, but he was out to falsify things; it was the first battle the Arab Liberation Army had fought, and defeat had to be turned into victory. And Ahmad Bey had cottoned on to this, thinking quickly and telling the deputy how our forces had taught those Jewish bastards a lesson they wouldn't forget—and how he'd seized a wonderful bullet-proof vest in the process.

At that point Najib had been struck dumb by amazement, unable to utter a word; and when he'd been ordered to put the vest in the deputy's car, he'd simply walked off with it instead, out onto the plain.

There, meeting fierce winds, he'd put the vest on over his clothes and walked on, not knowing where, except that he knew, instinctively, he was walking toward Lake Tiberias—toward his home town of Samakh.

On he'd walked, through that wild, dark night. His nose had frozen, and the tips of his fingers had grown stiff, but still he hadn't stopped. His steps had gotten heavier; he'd fallen in ditches, stumbled over rocks and heard, within the folds of the night, the winds howling, whistling and wailing. He was exhausted, but he fought on. He walked and walked, seeing, in those plains, no light and no glimpse of a man. At last he couldn't go on any longer. Everything in him had frozen or grown stiff. Only his heart had gone on beating under that wonderful armor.

Suddenly he'd fallen and passed out, only waking in the hospital, after some shepherds had found him at dawn next day. When he'd recovered he'd asked about the vest, and they'd told him it was being kept safe.

When it was time for him to leave for Qatanna, he'd gone to the soldier responsible and asked for it. The soldier had looked furtively around him, then whispered: "Forget you ever saw it. Just thank God Ahmad Bey didn't call you to account for what you did."

And so the bullet-proof vest had gone its way – vanished. Najib tried to put it out of his mind, but at the end of the evening, when we'd gone through all our various stories and I'd started yawning, Najib stood for a long time at the window staring out. Perhaps he was watching the clouds gathering in the sky, or listening to the murmur of the Barada's waters; or maybe he was listening for the call of that mighty armor.

When he woke next morning, his eyes were puffy and his face was pale and tired. He obviously hadn't slept much that night. We went down to the restaurant for breakfast, and, as we drank our tea, Najib tried his best to seem normal and cheerful. I regaled him with an amusing story, and he replied with one that was ironic and even bitter. Suddenly my gaze was drawn to the doors of the hotel.

There, in the entrance, stood a woman wrapped in a black cloak, her face covered by a light veil. She was tall and slim. Najib saw my amazed look.

"Do you know her?" he asked.

I made to get up, but she'd already turned and left. I got up and hurried after her, but she was already disappearing. I gazed intently after her, but couldn't make out whether her palms were henna-dyed or not.

Chapter Four

The yellow Ford spluttered on for a mile or so, then came to a halt.

The sun's disk dipped down behind the hills, and the hilltop loomed large against the sky. There were no birds to be seen now; there was just the smell of grass and a sound of chirping from the inner branches of a big wild carob tree.

The car stopped, even though Hamid Abu Hamid had recited *Ayat al-Kursi** and Abd al-Karim al-Hamad had invoked all the righteous ones to keep the vehicle moving.

As the spluttering started, Hamid Abu Hamid scowled, realizing the motor was going to let him down here in the middle of nowhere, where no one passed at night. He kept pressing on the accelerator, which made the car jerk forward for a moment before it started dying again.

Abd al-Karim scanned Hamid's face, but saw only a scowl that made his heart sink. He fingered the money belt around his waist,

---

* *Ayat al-Kursi*: A Quranic verse recited to implore Divine aid.

still hopeful Abu Hamid might find some solution. Then, after a further struggle, the car came to a stop and died completely.

Abu Hamid gave a deep sigh, bitterness and fury written all over his face. Abd al-Karim tried to say something.

"Be quiet a minute, man," Abu Hamid snapped.

Abu Hamid wasn't the kind of man to get worked up for no good reason, and it was then Abd al-Karim al-Hamad realized how very serious the situation was. He said nothing, but just watched as Abu Hamid got out of the car and tried to open the hood in the front, before quickly pulling back his hand. It must have been burning hot. He took out his handkerchief, and, when he finally got the hood open, compressed steam hissed out of it. He stood back, waiting for it to clear a little, then came up to the window.

"Sorry, Abd al-Karim," he said, more quietly now. "Come out and get a breath of air."

Realizing his friend had calmed down, Abd al-Karim felt a surge of sympathy and swallowed any resentment he'd felt. Then he opened the door and got out, to the scent of grass, the smell of open country, and the sound of birds, and desolation as far as the eye could see.

"I'll have to wait for the engine to cool down," Abu Hamid said.

There was only a faint tone of hope in his voice. He was steeling himself to face this sudden setback.

Abd al-Karim had spent two days traveling around the bedouin encampments, trying to collect his debts. He'd managed to collect about a hundred guineas, mostly in coins that he'd stuffed into the money belt around his waist, over the precious jeweled dagger he wore not for defense or attack, but simply as an ornament.

Of course the car had to go wrong just as night was falling! Abu Hamid once more lifted the hood and leaned over to examine the engine, while Abd al-Karim looked out over the landscape.

To the left was farm land and to the right a big carob tree, beyond which the land rose gradually to form a hill dotted with thorny plants. There was a shepherd walking up the hill opposite with his flock, the bell on the ram sending out a monotonous ringing sound. As for the dirt road, used by cars and animals alike, it was empty and silent.

How far away Samakh seemed at moments like this!

He went up to Abu Hamid, who was still bending over the engine, but said nothing. He didn't dare ask anything; he just waited for some sign of hope. What was taking Abu Hamid so long? When would he lift his head, give a little smile, and say: "It's okay now." When?

But when, after a long wait, he did lift his head, his features were stony.

"There's nothing we can do," Abd al-Karim said, dejected now. "We'll have to spend the night here."

"Well, what do you have to worry about?" Abu Hamid immediately rejoined. "You haven't got any wife or children waiting for you."

He bit his lip, immediately regretting what he'd said. Did he really have to remind Abd al-Karim he lived alone now, since his wife passed on all those years ago, without even bearing him any children? But Abd al-Karim, who was pretty thick-skinned, took no notice.

"Isn't there any way out?" he asked quietly.

"Well," Abu Hamid answered, "it's not that late yet. You could walk it if you kept going. You'd make it for the dawn prayers. Or," he went on, "you could look for a place to sleep with the shepherds, on the other side of those hills."

"And what about you?" Abd al-Karim asked, in a gentler voice.

"I can't leave my car."

Abd al-Karim hesitated, going over the options in his mind. Should he walk to Samakh? Or try and find shelter behind those hills?

He was daunted by the distances involved and, in any case, knew nothing of these roads. The whole thing was fraught with danger; these were anxious times and the country was at war. He tried to picture what it would be like spending the night there.

Abu Hamid came up to him.

"Think of it as one of those summer nights," he said reassuringly. "When you sleep out in the fields." But he was anxious even so.

Still Abd al-Karim couldn't make up his mind. He walked around, exploring the spot. He contemplated the carob tree, then, feeling an instinctive need for open space, started climbing the hill. What he saw there made him cry out.

Abu Hamid came running up to him. The slope was a low one.

"Look," Abd al-Karim said. He pointed to some lights in the distance.

Abu Hamid, seriously worried now, turned to go back.

"It's a Jewish settlement," he said.

It was pitch black now, and the birds had all fallen silent. Abd al-Karim felt a hideous shock pass through him; then, demoralized, he turned and dragged himself down the hill. The darkness was all but complete. Even a small tree looked like a giant shadow, and the little thorn bushes had become black spots. You couldn't see your own hand in front of your face.

"Do you want to walk?" Abu Hamid asked.

He was only joking. He went to the back of the car and took out a mat, a prayer rug, a water bottle, a box of food and a loaf of bread.

"Have some of this food, go on. My wife prepared it, and I haven't even started it. We'll share."

"I'm not hungry," Abd al-Karim said. He'd had a good meal before starting out.

"I'll leave your share, then. It'll be a long night. You'll get hungry some time."

A cold breeze sprang up while Abu Hamid was eating, making Abd al-Karim shiver.

"Have a drink," Abu Hamid said. Abd al-Karim took the water bottle and drank, almost choking in the process. He could feel his strength failing. The yellow car, standing nearby, looked black now.

In an attempt to give them both some courage, Abu Hamid suggested:

"Let's pray."

Abd al-Karim felt safer and more at peace after his prayers. Abu Hamid went off, then, after a while, came back carrying some dry wood and straw.

"Shall we light a fire?" he asked.

"Yes," Abd al-Karim answered. "You feel less lonely with a fire. What about those Jews, though? Do you think they might spot us if we light one?"

Abu Hamid thought it over. On a pitch dark night like this, a fire would light the whole place up, and that might attract the attention of the Jews in that settlement over there. They could send a patrol out to shoot at them. That was what was making him so anxious, and more and more perplexed.

"You're right," he said at last. "It's better not to."

He put down the bundle of firewood and sat on the edge of the mat.

You never know just what life's going to bring, Abd al-Karim said to himself. We certainly weren't expecting a night like this!

It's just one night, Abu Hamid thought, and it'll pass. Tomorrow the sun will come up, and the day has eyes.

"Our group spends the evenings at Haj Hussein's now," Abu Hamid said, trying to make conversation. He needed to say something, to break the silence. Abd al-Karim rarely spent the evening at his brother-in-law's, but he knew from his nephew Radi everything that went on there. He wasn't fond of late nights himself, preferring to go to bed early, but he listened attentively to Radi's reports of the war news they discussed there. Suddenly he missed Radi a lot.

"Our people from the National Committee are at Haj Hussein's now," Abu Hamid went on. "God only knows how they'll deal with the evacuation of the border force."

Abd al-Karim didn't know what to say. In fact it was the first time he'd heard anything at all of the matter. Abu Hamid, though, took an interest in every issue that came up, big or small, and didn't try and hide his sympathy with the Mufti. "Al-Taher's promised to come anyway," he added, more to reassure himself than his companion.

Al-Taher. Al-Taher. He'd left the town a year before to join the Mufti in Jerusalem, and he'd gone off on a training mission.

"He's working under Fawzi al-Qutub in the sabotage group," Abu Hamid said. "He's in Jerusalem on a secret mission."

"How do you know he'll come back to Samakh?" Abd al-Karim asked.

Abu Hamid talked, on and on, about al-Taher, recounting stories Abd al-Karim couldn't be sure were real or just a web of fancy. Al-Taher grew that night, filling the hills and the valley.

Slowly sleep was overcoming Abd al-Karim, his predicament forgotten, and Abu Hamid started yawning too. Hours had passed.

"I'm tired out," Abu Hamid said. "I think I'll sleep here. You can go sleep in the car if it gets too cold."

"I'm sleepy too," Abd al-Karim answered.

He took off his shoes, put them underneath his head and stretched out on the mat, while Abu Hamid stretched out on the prayer rug nearby, closed his eyes and, within a few minutes, started snoring.

Abd al-Karim started feeling afraid all over again. He was wide awake again now, thinking of all the possible disasters they might meet. The sound of the trees, the rustling of the leaves, grew louder in his brain. In the end he fell asleep from sheer exhaustion, but still went on tossing and turning, as though he was sleeping on thorns.

✖

Suddenly he opened his eyes. Was it a dream, or had he heard a movement, the faint sound of a stealthy footstep? The sound of breathing, from something that wasn't human? He opened his eyes, gripped totally by a fear that made his whole body shake and his hair stand up.

It was pitch dark, and there was a sting in the cold that chilled him to the bone. He got up. "Who's there?" he shouted, in a voice that wasn't like his own at all.

A large animal leaped up in front of him. He didn't see it, but felt its movement, or rather the direction of the leap from the sound it made landing on the grass. Perhaps the animal was standing there now, quite still. He seemed to see two bright eyes in the dark, accompanied by a fearful hissing.

Instinctively he stretched out his hand to take the dagger he'd never used before in his life, his fear tempered by the urge to defend himself. His voice had gone, as he thought; he was panic-stricken. Then, after a while, it occurred to him to wake Abu Hamid. He shook him violently and the other man started out of his sleep.

"In the name of God! What's the matter?"

"There's some dangerous animal just close by."

Abu Hamid jumped up, hurried to the boot of the car and took out the wrench he used every day to start up the car's fan. Then he stood at the ready.

"It's a hyena," he said. "A big one."

"Can you see it?" Abd al-Karim asked.

"No, but I know it's a hyena. I caught its smell."

Abu Hamid took a few steps forward. Where was it now?

"Maybe it's gone."

"If it's a hyena, it'll be back. You can be sure of that."

The two men were standing out there in the open, one frightened, the other pretending to be brave; both unable to act. A dreadful, overwhelming fear weighed down on them.

Abu Hamid drank a little water and wiped his face, while Abd al-Karim stood there with his hand on his dagger, wondering just how to go about it if he were forced to take the beast on.

"Sit down, Abd al-Karim," Abu Hamid said. "Let's try and think a bit. If it was a hyena, then it'll be back for sure. But if it was a wild pig, it'll just run off somewhere else."

"It was a filthy hyena. I'll bet you whatever you like!"

Within a few minutes Abd al-Karim's teeth were chattering, whether from fear or cold Abu Hamid couldn't tell. He thought of that pile of firewood he'd gathered, wondering whether to light a fire after all. It would warm them up and stop the hyena getting too close as well. They'd never come near a fire.

He took his lighter, and a spark flew, but there was no flame.

"What are you doing?" Abd al-Karim asked.

"I think we'd better light a fire after all," Abu Hamid said. He'd decided to take the risk to calm his friend down. Abd al-Karim seemed, though, to have regained some of his composure.

"Don't, for heaven's sake!" he said. "Have you forgotten that settlement close by?"

No, he hadn't. And he knew, too, that the danger from it hadn't passed. The hyena on one side and the Jews on the other. They were trapped between the two. He searched once more in the boot of the car, found the piece of cloth he occasionally used to lie on when he had to repair the engine, and placed it around Abd al-Karim's shoulders. It might give him a little protection against the cold.

Then he heard footfalls. A shudder passed through him, and he heard Abd al-Karim saying: "Did you hear that?"

Abu Hamid tried to work out which direction the beast was

coming from, but his senses failed him. Why was he holding his breath? Still he stood there waiting, as though there were a struggle going on between him and this creature using all its cunning.

The cloth fell from Abd al-Karim's shoulders, and the creature moved a step closer. Immediately Abu Hamid threw the metal wrench at it, with all the strength he could muster, and hit it. An indescribable howl sounded as the beast turned, and they heard the sound of its fleeing footsteps.

Abd al-Karim had been taken by surprise.

"What happened?" he said.

"It's gone and it won't be coming back. You'll be safe now."

How was he to feel safe? The night wasn't over yet; there was still plenty of time for the animal to come back before that first faint thread of light appeared. Still, what Abu Hamid had done had filled him with strength and confidence. He took the water bottle and drank, then wiped his face.

"As you've decided not to light the fire," Abd al-Karim said, "we'd be better off sleeping inside the car." That would be safer, he thought, because the beast wouldn't be able to break the car windows and come in.

They got in the car and closed the windows, Abu Hamid sitting in the front and Abd al-Karim in the back. They didn't speak; each was in his private world, sunk in his own fears and apprehensions.

Abd al-Karim was thinking about the hyena, recalling all the things he'd heard at Haj Hussein's receptions, in the old days before the war, when he still used to go there. The hyena knew its victim, it was said, among forty other men, only terrorizing the faint-hearted. It approached its victim, urinated on its tail, then splashed it in the victim's face, hypnotizing him. At that the victim would lose control of his will and run after the hyena to its cave. If the entrance to the cave was high, the victim would just pass through and the hyena would leap on him and eat him; but if the entrance was low, then the victim would beat his head against the rock and blood would flow from the wound. Then the victim would wake up, so to speak, and go back where he'd come from, and the hyena wouldn't dare follow him, because the hyena only ate people there in its cave. Those were the stories they kept telling, just a little different every night, about hyenas.

Abu Hamid, for his part, wasn't thinking about hyenas. It would soon be light now and the beasts would all flee to their dens. And soon the settlement tractors would be out to plow the fields. What would happen to them if there were Palmach men in the settlement, who wouldn't hesitate to shoot anyone who passed?

When will it be dawn? Abd al-Karim kept asking himself. Then the hyena will go back to its den.

Looking out of the car window into the darkness beyond, he seemed to see a still darker mass approaching from one side, with piercing eyes, and another from the other side. He could almost hear the sound of footsteps running over the brush. As for Abu Hamid, he felt tired; and, resting his head on the back of his seat, he fell asleep in spite of everything. Soon he was snoring loudly once more.

Abd al-Karim, wide awake now, scanning the dark and prey to every imaginable fear, felt a sudden need to pass water. There was enormous pressure on his bladder. Should he open the door and get out, go and relieve himself despite all his terrors?

He thought of waking Abu Hamid but couldn't bring himself to do it. Must he be so weak and ruled by fear?

He opened the door, put out his right leg and waited a little. Then he cocked his ears. There was no sound except for the sound of the wind in the carob trees. He got out of the car, his hand firmly on the hilt of his dagger, his whole body on the alert.

He took a few steps behind the car, breathing in the night air. It was refreshing, soaked with dew. He unbuttoned his trousers and, as he urinated, the pressure on his bladder eased, bringing him a great sense of relief. He felt he needed to take in some more fresh air.

Then, suddenly, he heard the hyena and something that sounded like pots banging. The hyena, he realized, was searching for remnants of food in the container; the smell of food had drawn it, perhaps, and aroused its lust for blood.

He stood still, his hand on his dagger, gripped by terror. Then he heard another sound, from a new direction this time, and a shudder passed right through him. These animals would, he realized, go to any length to get their prey.

Abu Hamid was apparently roused by all the noise.

"Where are you, Abd al-Karim?" he called out. He got out of the car. "Where are you?" he called again.

Abd al-Karim said something unintelligible, but which showed, nevertheless, where he was. A big group of hyenas was there, making frightful noises, intent on getting their prey. The car wasn't safe any more, because the hungry animals wouldn't hesitate to break in through the windows.

"What are we going to do?" Abd al-Karim asked faintly.

"We'll have to make a fire," Abu Hamid answered. "There's no other way."

"But—" Abd al-Karim began, in the same weak voice. Abu Hamid interrupted him loudly.

"Are we just going to stay here in the dark and be eaten by hyenas?"

Right away, he flicked his lighter and bent over the firewood, and the beasts drew back a little at the sudden sparks. Within seconds the dry leaves and twigs had caught fire and a thick smoke was rising. The hyenas retreated further and further.

"I'm not going to stand by and let them eat us," Abu Hamid shouted.

The flames got higher, as the fire caught the wood on all sides. The place was lit up now, and the sight of Abu Hamid revived Abd al-Karim's courage. Still the light spread. The carob tree appeared, its shadow spreading far and wide, and the car became visible, along with the empty food container and the mat and the prayer rug; and they could see one another.

The thick darkness had melted away, and the beasts had gone too. Still, though, their fears kept growing.

"What if the Jews in that settlement find us?" Abd al-Karim asked.

"Well anyway," Abu Hamid answered, "we won't die like cowards." He went on feeding the fire with whatever he could find.

The whole valley and all the hills were lit up by it. Abd al-Karim climbed to the top of a hill overlooking the settlement and came hurrying back, his heart pounding violently. "The lights of the settlement have been turned off," he said. "Maybe they've seen we're here."

Abu Hamid leaned on the front of the car.

"They'll wait until dawn," he said. "And then we can set off ourselves, without any worry about animals."

The only thing worse than a wild beast, Abd al-Karim thought, is the human beast. "If only we had some sort of weapon," he said. "If only we had a rifle to defend ourselves with."

Abu Hamid remembered the wrench and went in search of it in the thick grass, while Abd al-Karim closed his eyes and vowed to buy a rifle if they got safely through the night.

When Abu Hamid came back with the wrench, he said:

"How much does a French rifle cost? An Umm Habba?"

He fingered the money belt, which he'd almost forgotten now. At the same moment a mass of flames rose high on a nearby hilltop.

"Look!" Abd al-Karim cried, in amazement and confusion. The fire almost lit up the sky. "What's going on?"

Abu Hamid didn't answer, but just went on watching the hill.

"Perhaps there are shepherds there," Abd al-Karim went on. "Maybe they've been attacked by hyenas. Or surrounded by wolves."

Still Abu Hamid said nothing, waiting.

Another fire appeared, on another hill. All kinds of emotions played over Abu Hamid's face. Then joy burst through them, and he cried:

"God is great!"

Abd al-Karim approached in astonishment, as though witnessing a miracle.

"It's a signal, from the shepherds on the hills just over there."

In his joy Abd al-Karim could see the lake growing ever bigger, with the white birds fluttering over it. His hand was still on the hilt of his dagger.

"We're not alone any more, are we?" Abu Hamid whispered.

Abd al-Karim had regained his nerve. He felt at peace now, his heart restored to him, for dawn was approaching. Fear and anxiety had been replaced by a longing for his house and garden, and the sight of Fatima and Qassem al-Nayyef, and he thought fondly of a nap on his big brass bed.

As the fire died down, leaving just embers behind it, the sun burst up, birds started singing and Abu Hamid stood by the side of the road waiting for the bus to take him to Tiberias. Abd al-Karim asked once more:

"You didn't answer my question. How much does a French rifle cost?"

"What?" Abu Hamid said. "You mean you're actually thinking of buying one?"

The bus appeared at last, driven by Abu Samra. His face peered out from behind the front window, the swarthy face with the glasses perched on top of his nose and the white hair that showed his age. He stopped and greeted them, without getting down, while the peasants looked on.

"Have you spent the night here?" he said. "God forgive you!"

He opened the door and, without waiting for further explanation, went to get the rope from the back.

They were both weary—pitifully exhausted in fact. Soon, though, they were in the car, being towed along by the bus, while the peasants kept turning around to stare at them.

The sides of the bus were decorated with drawings and etchings, like the ones put on house gates to ward off the evil eye. As for the phrases written on the glass, they expressed thanks to the Creator, who bestowed good fortune on whom He wished.

Time passed slowly, but everything went smoothly, and at last they could make out Tiberias in the distance.

"There's Tiberias," Abu Hamid said, and Abd al-Karim gazed through heavy eyes. How near Samakh was now! A breeze stirred from the lake, the lake that provided a living, that granted life to man, bird and plant.

The streets of Tiberias were thronged, full of cars, vendors, carts and bicycles. There was cloth and silver and brass; glass and porcelain; jewelry, bracelets and rings; the fish market, boats, and cats looking for food. A flock of white birds flew in a curve along the shore, and there were all kinds of faces, Arab and Jew, and British police cars.

The bus stopped at Maarouf's garage. Then Abu Samra untied the rope, wished them goodbye and went off with his peasants to the town center.

Chapter Five

The car came to a halt in front of a large house set in its garden. "Thank God for your safe arrival," Abu Hamid said. "God willing, I'll see you fit and well tomorrow."

Abd al-Karim got out of the car, to be greeted by the maidservant Fatima, who was carrying a bunch of *farfahina*.* She must have just cut them, because they were still covered in dew.

"Welcome home, Uncle," she said. "God be praised for your safe arrival."

Fatima had grown up in this house, which was called "The House of Peace." She'd come from the village of al-Mukhaiba as a child and was one of the family now. The House of Peace had been prosperous in those days, the father vigorous, the mother in perfect health and Abd al-Karim's wife Munira glowing like a candle. As for Radi's mother Khadijeh, she'd still been in elementary school, her red ribbon showing through her braid.

The big house had been alive then with the vibrant presence of the family, along with guests and visitors. It hadn't had to face

* *Farfahina*: A plant with fleshy leaves, used mainly in salads.

any tragedies yet. Fatima had grown up in the old house, and had called Abd al-Karim "Uncle" since she was a child.

Now everyone had gone. Khadijeh had married, and there was no one left in the House of Peace except him, together with the old chairs made from engraved wood and velvet cloth, the Persian carpets, the Damascene curtains and the brass bed.

Fatima put the *farfahina* on a mat under the vine and took out the big house key.

"The house is cleaned," she said. "I thought you'd be coming today somehow, so I cleaned and washed. It's all spotless, like snow."

Her husband Qassem al-Nayyef came up with a rake. He'd been clearing the channel that irrigated the eggplant patch, which was covered with violet flowers now.

"Your coming's only brought good, Uncle," he said.

Abd al-Karim really felt he was home now, for these two were the last ones left in the big house. They looked after the house and garden, sleeping in an annex in the garden. He took the key.

"Will you eat with us, Uncle?" Fatima asked.

He wasn't hungry and his eyes were heavy with sleep.

"I'm going straight to bed," he said.

He opened the door, went in, hid the money in the cupboard, then sank into a long, deep sleep. He had some terrible dreams, all jumbled up together, but when he woke he couldn't remember any of them. The sun was about to set, and the sound of the cows told him the cowherd had come back from the pasture.

He had a drink from a clay jug and got dressed for the evening in his cream *rosa*[*] gown and Damascene cloak. Then he put on his belt, with the jeweled dagger at his side, and went out into the garden. Fatima was leading the black and white cow, which had

[*] *Rosa*: An imported pure silk of off-white color, traditionally used for formal wear by men of means.

just come back, its udders swollen with milk.

Abd al-Karim sat down on a mat under the trees in the orchard, which was strung with hanging okra and dried red peppers. Qassem al-Nayyef was tinkering with the motor that pumped water up from the lake, because it was better to water in the evening. As the engine came to life, the birds flew off and chickens and rabbits scattered, and the water started rising in the reservoir. Through all the noise of the engine, the voice of Abu Adnan al-Zabadneh could be heard, raised high in the evening call to prayer.

"Blessed is the name of God," Abd al-Karim said to himself. He rose, performed his ablutions and prayed, after which Fatima arrived with a bowl of milk.

"God be praised and protect us from the evil eye," she said, "there's more cream than milk."

He took the bowl and drank deeply. When Fatima had gone, Qassem al-Nayyef came up with a lantern, which he hung at the edge of the orchard. Then he squatted down, his eyes on the jeweled dagger Abd al-Karim wore on special occasions.

"Do you like the dagger, Qassem?" Abd al-Karim asked mischievously.

"Yes, by God. That precious green stone especially."

Abd al-Karim took out the dagger. What a superbly curved blade, and what a superb hilt, fitting perfectly in the hand.

"Its a wonderful dagger," Qassem said. "I bet you had it specially made, Uncle."

They could hear Fatima's voice calling the chickens to roost.

What would he think, Abd al-Karim wondered, as he put the dagger back in its sheath, if he knew I was going to buy a rifle?

"If I go to Damascus," he said, "I'll buy you one like it."

Having fed the chickens, Fatima closed the door of the coop and turned her attention to the *taboun** oven, which she filled with

* *Taboun*: A closed oven in which bread, chicken, etc. may be cooked.

firewood and lit. Next she uncovered the basin whose dough was filling the place with its aroma. Then, squatting on the mat, she asked her husband:

"Did you tell him Radi came while he was asleep?"

He clapped his hands.

"God shame the devil! I forgot to tell you, Uncle, Radi and Khaled al-Zaher came asking for you while you were asleep. Haj Hussein will be expecting you tonight at his reception."

The fire in the *taboun* was going strongly now, and reflected off Fatima's face, making her cheeks look like red apples.

"Saddle the mare for me," Abd al-Karim said. Qassem got up.

"The shepherds went off to Haj Hussein's lands in Umm al-Masari yesterday," he said as he left. "For the harvest season."

Abd al-Karim's thoughts wandered. The harvest season was coming, there in the low-lying parts of the valley. The ears of grain would be full of seeds, and at Umm al-Masari summer would have struck suddenly. Even so, it was early. Haj Hussein was a man of good intentions and God gave to him accordingly. His spacious lands were bountiful, giving food to birds and travelers.

At harvest time he got help from all the peasants. Some came to reap and some to gather up the grain, while others still came to work the threshing floor. Behind them came the poor people who gleaned the ears of grain the gatherers had dropped, or which had escaped the reapers' scythes. And behind them again came the animals, who ate until their stomachs were ready to burst.

Abd al-Karim wasn't thinking, any more, about the debts he'd been so intent on collecting. After that terrifying night spent far from his home, he just wanted to fling his arms wide and embrace something in the small town.

The smell of freshly baked bread wafted over to him and he felt like eating some; and Fatima, seeing him looking at her, guessed this and handed him a loaf that had just come smoking out of the *taboun*. He ate it with immense relish, and was just going to ask for another one when Qassem came, leading by the reins the white mare he paraded so proudly on Fridays and public holidays, and when the horsemen raced to al-Shifa.

The mare had been eating straw and vetch all day, so that her body was taut, her neck high and graceful as a gazelle's. Abd al-Karim took hold of the neck and, with a single bound, was on her back. He pulled in the reins, then loosened them and, since she was a thoroughbred, left her to make her own way.

He crossed the farm path, then went on alongside the railway tracks, passing in front of Tadrus's mill and then the boat house, before riding through the empty alleys to Haj Hussein's house. The small door of the gate opened, and Khaled al-Zaher peered out, then hurried to take the mare's reins.

"Haj Hussein's gone to the National Committee," he said. "He won't be long."

Abd al-Karim knew he'd arrived early. He left Khaled al-Zaher to look after the mare and went into the courtyard, where Wolf was lying asleep. Radi peered out of the attic window.

"Uncle!" he cried. "Welcome." He turned and rushed down to embrace him.

This boy's like a part of myself, Abd al-Karim thought. Radi opened the doors to the reception room, switched on the light and ushered his uncle in. The room was suffused with the smell of incense and the aromas of coffee and cardamom, and the water in the jar was mixed with orange blossom essence and lemon leaves. Everything was in its place: the cushions and rugs and seats; the mortar and pestle, and the roaster, and the Arabic brass coffee pots.

Abd al-Karim sat down in a suitable place. It was a long while since he'd been here and drunk the bitter coffee mixed with ginger or cardamom. He sat there, or rather reclined. Opposite him sat Radi, gazing at the clothes he so rarely wore and the dagger at his side. Khadijeh, Radi's mother, came down from the attic, announced by the telltale noise of her wooden clogs on the tile stairs.

She peered around the door in her long-sleeved dress and white headdress, but didn't come in.

"Praise God you're safely back, brother," she said.

Abd al-Karim got up to shake her hand. Little Khadijeh had grown up. She'd become a mother and her tenderness had grown too.

He went back to his seat while she stayed standing there at the door, unable to come in. The men might come back suddenly, who knew, and it wasn't fitting for women to go in where men were holding forth.

"Pour some coffee for your uncle, son," she said.

Radi stood up and offered the coffee in the proper way. First he swilled out the cup with a little coffee, which he threw out. Next he poured out some more, which he tasted to make sure everything was all right. Then he poured out a third cup for his uncle.

Khadijeh took the packet of money from her pocket.

"Radi ran the shop yesterday and today," she said, "but there wasn't much business."

Abd al-Karim thanked her and took the packet, thinking, with a sense of security, of the sums he'd managed to collect. It was a good thing to have money in the hand these days. Who could tell what the future might bring?

Khadijeh left them. She could hear the baby, Maher, crying, and went back upstairs while Radi stayed talking with his uncle. Abd al-Karim asked the questions and Radi answered, speaking like a boy who wanted to grow up before his time.

"We stayed up until dawn yesterday—we saw the reapers and harvesters off—my aunt Hafiza went to the Duwair farm."

Abd al-Karim was picturing it all. He could see the sacks of grain, the jars of fat, the piles of wool. But would people find the quiet, the peace of mind, to see the season through?

"That dagger really suits you, Uncle," Radi said.

It was an old dagger he'd inherited from his father, and for a long time it had lain neglected in the cupboard, until finally the silver had darkened. Then, when he'd decided to wear it again, for reasons of pride and decoration, he'd sent it to the shop of Asad al-Khanjar, the jeweler, who'd polished it and cleaned the green gem until it gleamed like a star in the sky. He wondered, as before: What would my nephew think if he knew I was going to buy a rifle?

A mighty din broke out suddenly in the courtyard. Haj Hussein had come back, bringing his guests with him. He came in with his cane, followed by the others, and Abd al-Karim sprang up to greet him, and to greet Sheikh Mustafa al-Sanusi, the Circassian, Salim al-Aid, Mansour, the ticket seller in the train station, and a stranger in military uniform. There was a long rifle hanging from Haj Hussein's shoulder.

"This is our brother-in-law, Abd al-Karim," the Haj said. "And this," he went on, pointing to the officer, "is Ahmad Bey. He's a commander in the Arab Liberation Army."

There was a pall of gloom over the faces of everyone there, following that long-drawn-out meeting in the offices of the National Committee. Why was everyone so gloomy, Abd al-Karim wondered? God be merciful!

They sat down, and Khaled al-Zaher served coffee to everyone. Abd al-Karim couldn't keep his eyes off the rifle Haj Hussein had taken from his shoulder now and placed in his lap. Radi whispered to his uncle, gesturing toward Ahmad Bey. He was eager to hear how things had gone with the navy blue bullet-proof vest. Abd al-Karim was curious too, but he couldn't find a proper moment to ask.

At the meeting the men had a long discussion about an expected attack by the Jews on the small town, and they carried on with this at the reception. By the time the meeting was over, the elders of the town, and the dignitaries and the young men who owned rifles, were all on the alert. Ahmad Bey, who'd come in response to a request from the National Committee—in a military car this time, along with two guards—had advised the meeting to send a delegation to the Commander, Fawzi al-Kawuqji, at his headquarters in the village of Jaba.

"Time's running out for us, Ahmad Bey," the Haj said. "No one knows what's going to happen from one day to the next."

Ahmad Bey glanced at his watch, stood up, pulled himself erect and said he had to leave.

"You haven't answered us, Ahmad Bey," said the Haj.

Ahmad Bey said once more he had to go back to Beisan, as things were getting dangerous. He started pressing them, in various ways, to send the delegation to see al-Kawuqji. Abd al-Karim felt the fear stirring deep inside him. The men's eyes were all glued to Ahmad Bey's face.

Salim al-Aid spoke, then Sheikh Mustafa, then Mansour, all to the same effect as Haj Hussein. Radi was fidgeting. He would have liked to be allowed to ask about two things: the vest, and Najib, who'd volunteered for the Liberation Army.

Ahmad Bey nodded.

"Very well," he said. "As soon as I get back, I'll send a message to the Commander, to tell him how things are in Samakh."

"We need weapons, Ahmad Bey."

"Well, I'll send the message."

He had nothing more to say and was escorted to the door by Haj Hussein, who returned grim-faced. As Khaled al-Zaher served more coffee, Radi whispered to his uncle, making his heart beat fearfully. Then the men started leaving, enjoined by Haj Hussein to be on the alert, until only the Circassian, who was usually the last to leave, remained. Feeling sleepy, he'd stretched out and closed his eyes.

Haj Hussein turned to his brother-in-law.

"Listen, Abd al-Karim," he said, in a serious voice. "You must stay with us tonight. Your house is lonely, and it's in a farming area close to the Jews. Do you follow me?"

Abd al-Karim's heart sank, and once again he was struck by fear.

He could see, in his imagination, the hyenas' fangs, and feel the dark forms approaching him.

"Your house is on the outskirts," the Haj was saying. "We've already warned everyone living in the isolated parts to take precautions or go and stay with relatives or friends in the town. We're expecting an attack from the Jews. Do you understand?"

He slung the rifle over his shoulder and went out, while Radi looked at his uncle, noticing how pale and agitated his face had become.

"It's a chance for you to sleep here with us," he said playfully. "I'll read you one of the chronicles of Abu Hilal."

Abd al-Karim couldn't help smiling at his nephew. Radi got up, went to the cupboard in the wall and fetched the tale of Antara al-Absi.

"Shall I read you the tale of Antara?" he asked.

"Let's leave it for another time," Abd al-Karim said absently.

The Circassian opened his eyes and peered around. Then, seeing the others had gone, he adjusted his clothes and asked for another cup of coffee, which Radi poured for him. He downed it in two gulps, then asked Abd al-Karim:

"Did you manage to collect your debts from the Subeih bedouins?"

But Abd al-Karim was a man of few words, and he was pondering the disasters lurking beyond the firmly bolted gates. Suddenly they heard the whine of one of those amphibious planes that came to the border guards' camp. The noise got louder and louder, until finally it seemed directly overhead.

"It's never come as late as this before," Radi said.

The Circassian nodded. "It's all for the best, God willing," he said. "All for the best."

Haj Hussein came back, announced by the tap of his stick, and entered the room with the rifle slung over his shoulder. He'd brought it two weeks before from the Druze Mountain and carried it proudly now. He sat down and began to speak.

"The British have started leaving," he said. "They'll be out of the police headquarters tonight." He poured himself a cup of coffee.

"The Jews will try and get to it before we do," the Circassian broke in.

So, there was a solid basis for all that speculation! Abd al-Karim leaped up.

"I'm going home," he said. He was thinking of Fatima and Qassem al-Nayyef.

Radi clung to his uncle's arm.

"Your house is near the Ofakim settlement," he said. "Who knows—"

"Listen, Radi," the Haj broke in. "Your uncle knows what's best for him. We must let him make up his own mind."

Abd al-Karim left, bowed down by his anxieties. His mare was tethered by the main gate, and he leaped onto her back and guided her through the alleys until they reached open ground, where she started flying like the wind.

The breeze from the lake reached him, but the smell borne on it was different now—the smell of dead weed, and smoke, and sulphur boiling deep in the ground. The smell of the night before still stank in his nostrils too, and he could see the movement of the hyenas, feel their stealthy danger and the sudden swirls of howling wind. Now, in this silence broken only by the patter of hooves on soil and the panting of the mare, Abd al-Karim felt a shudder that filled every cranny of the darkness.

When he arrived, Qassem al-Nayyef was waiting for him with a lantern in his hand. He hadn't heard the news and had felt no misgivings. As Abd al-Karim dismounted, he took the reins and went off to the stables. Halfway to the house Fatima was there with another lantern.

"Shall I get you some supper, Uncle?" she asked. Her voice was like the voice of a gazelle that's never been hunted.

"No. I'm not hungry."

Fatima lit the way to the house, the lantern raised high above her head. When they'd got in, she lit the candelabra and wished him goodnight. Abd al-Karim mumbled something back, closed the door behind her and took off his cloak. Then he stood in the middle of the big sitting room, thinking.

He hadn't decided what to do yet; he was acting on instinct. He hurried over to the wardrobe, took the money hidden in the drawer and wrapped it in a nylon bag. Then he wrapped this in a piece of cloth, went out into the garden and started digging.

Qassem al-Nayyef came over with his lantern.

"What are you doing, Uncle?" he asked. "Can I help?"

"Shshsh. Don't say anything. Just wait."

He waited as Abd al-Karim dug a hole and put in the bundle he was carrying. Abd al-Karim smoothed the soil back over it, then stood up, panting.

"Listen, Qassem al-Nayyef," he said. "If anything happens to me, this is where I've buried my money." With that he turned to go back to the house.

"Are you all right , Uncle?" Qassem al-Nayyef asked.

"Yes, of course I'm all right. I'm fine."

Fatima had already gone to bed. Qassem al-Nayyef was feeling sleepy himself, and hoped to cuddle up by her side before she was fast asleep.

"Do you need anything else, Uncle?" he asked.

Abd al-Karim's fears were growing. This, he knew, was Qassem's last question before going off to bed. What should he tell him? Should he be open and plant fear in his heart? The night might pass, after all, without the expected assault, so why scare him? There wasn't a rifle in the whole place, just a cudgel Qassem kept to use against thieves and foxes. If there'd only been a rifle in the House of Peace, he might have felt reassured.

Qassem was still standing there, his mind far away.

"Be on the alert tonight," Abd al-Karim said briefly. "There's a chance we may be attacked by thieves. Remember to untie the dogs and let them roam in the gardens."

Qassem al-Nayyef laughed. He didn't really know what fear was. He'd spent his whole life in the midst of darkness and the wilderness, and that bold heart of his had become like a lump of lead. Why should he be afraid of thieves?

"Don't worry, Uncle," he said. "Good night."

He turned and went off with his lantern, followed by the gnats, which always hover around light.

Abd al-Karim locked the door securely, then, turning around, caught a glimpse of himself in the mirror of the open cupboard. There was soil clinging to his clothes, and he still had the dagger at his side. He shook off the soil, then said:

"If only there was a rifle!"

He stretched out on the brass bed, only to be assailed by fears: the fears of the previous night, the fears of the last few months. He lay there sleepless, as though he were lying on thorns. The worries flared up inside him, with no hope of relief.

For an instant he thought of fleeing to the town, taking Fatima and Qassem with him, but a moment later dismissed the idea. He went on worrying, listening to every sound outside: each rustle of a tree, each rattle of a window, each howl of a distant dog, the sound of the ferry from Tiberias. He tossed and turned, now onto his left side, now onto his right, till he was worn out. But still sleep wouldn't come.

Suddenly he heard the noise of an explosion. A bomb had fallen somewhere on the town. Another explosion followed, rattling the window panes. Then a burst of gunfire.

It was the battle. It had come at last.

He was still trying to make out where the action was when there was a sudden knock at the door. He called out in alarm, his heart shrinking.

"Who's there?"

"It's me, Uncle," Fatima answered. She sounded close to tears.

He got up, still dressed, with the dagger at his side. The lantern, its oil exhausted, was sputtering its last. He opened the door, and Fatima came in trembling.

"Did you hear the sound of shooting, Uncle?" she said.

Her own fear communicated itself to him, but he tried to hold himself together.

"Don't be afraid, Fatima," he said. "It's a long way off."

Still she was trembling.

"Where's Qassem?" he asked.

"I don't know. He took the cudgel and went out. Maybe he's going to the stable first, or else around the orchard."

"That's all right then. Sit down."

The lantern was still lit, though black smoke was coming from it. "Sit down, Fatima," he said again. "Don't worry."

"I'll put some oil in the lantern," she said.

She took the lantern and went off to the kitchen, leaving the room plunged in darkness. He couldn't see a thing. The shooting was still going on—a long way off. He tried once more to pinpoint the place where the battle was raging. From what they'd said at the Haj's reception, he guessed the Jews were trying to occupy the police headquarters the British had left.

Soon Fatima came back, the hand with the lantern shaking. The room was flooded with light, and with something like reassurance too. She put the lantern in its place, then squatted down on the rug. He could see her disheveled hair now, and her black dress which, in her confusion, she'd put on inside out. As he sat down on the chair, his hand slipped instinctively onto the handle of the dagger, and this gave him a little courage.

Qassem al-Nayyef's voice came in through the window.

"Uncle, open up."

Fatima leaped up and opened the door, scanning her husband's face eagerly.

"Did you see anything, Qassem?" she asked confusedly. "Are they far away? Tell us. Why don't you say something?"

He came in with his stout stick and his lantern.

"Calm down, Fatima," he said. "The shooting's a long way from here. The Jews are attacking the town."

Abd al-Karim said nothing, and it was Qassem who finally broke the long silence.

"Fatima," he said. "If our uncle doesn't mind, go and make us a pot of tea."

She went out. Out in the orchard the dogs were barking, in a different way from anything Qassem had heard before. It was really getting on his nerves.

"Suppose the Jews succeed, Uncle," he said. "What will they do to us?"

"Listen, Qassem," Abd al-Karim answered, nervous and irritable. "This isn't the time, God guide you, for talking nonsense."

Qassem said no more, choking back all the questions he wanted to ask. When Fatima came back, he immediately poured out the tea, which they drank in silence. After about an hour the shooting was over except for the odd shot. The dogs started to calm down.

Qassem al-Nayyef couldn't restrain himself any longer and got ready to go out.

"What did I tell you?" he said. "Our people have thrown them back."

"Where are you going, Qassem?" Fatima asked.

"Out to the orchards," he said hurriedly. "To see if I can pick up some news."

Silence fell again. Abd al-Karim leaned back in his chair and stared at the ceiling, while Fatima stayed pensively on the rug, resting her face on her hand.

Suddenly a whole medley of sounds reached them. Something was approaching from the distance, from somewhere beyond the fields of crops and the brambles and the straw. The dogs started barking again, and panic took stealthy hold of them.

"What was that, Uncle?" Fatima said. "Did you hear it?"

"Keep calm, Fatima, keep calm," he said, in a terrified voice he didn't recognize as his own. Fatima, not reassured, got up and rushed over to the window.

"Can you see anything?" he said pleadingly, still not moving.

Beyond the window was only darkness. Fatima turned around.

"Go and hide, Uncle," she said. "I'm afraid for you, and for Qassem and me."

Voices could be heard, coming nearer and nearer, as if from just outside the window. Then he was able to make them out. They were Arabs—their own people.

"Can you hear, Uncle?" Fatima asked. "Are they from our town?"

This time light pierced in from outside. It was Qassem al-Nayyef's lantern. Fatima opened the door, and Qassem came in laughing.

"The Jews have lost the battle," he said. "Our men are chasing what's left of them. They're looking for the ones who went back along the farm track, to the al-Mallaha settlement."

Everything was peaceful again, peaceful and tranquil. The dogs had stopped barking and slowly they were calming down.

"According to the men who came by here," Qassem said, "the Jews had heavy losses and had to fall back and scatter."

Abd al-Karim recited the Fatiha verse from the Quran, then wiped his face with his hands. Fatima started yawning.

"Come on," Qassem said. "Let's go to bed. You look tired too, Uncle."

"Goodnight, Uncle," Fatima said sleepily.

She went out, followed by Qassem al-Nayyef with the lantern, and Abd al-Karim was alone. He stayed there, staring out of the window, until late in the night. Then, when he heard Sheikh Abu Hawwa's deep voice raised in the dawn call to prayer, he felt suddenly drowsy, went to his room and stretched out on his big brass bed.

Suddenly he heard the sound of a single shot, followed by a scream that split his heart in two. A human scream, for help. He felt as though the ground was heaving beneath him, and almost lost his balance. It had been a high-pitched, terrified scream.

Where did he get the courage? He leaped up and found himself at the door, then, as he ran toward the sound, he realized it had been Fatima's voice. He knew, too, that he had to do something, because her life was threatened in some way. Still he ran on, aware, suddenly, that the dagger was at his side. In the early dawn light he could smell the scents of grass and dew and terror, all rolled into one. He heard the barking of the chained-up dogs.

Halfway there, he heard another scream piercing the air, as though it had risen up from the depths of the earth. The dogs barked still more furiously, vainly trying to break free from their chains. He surged forward and came face to face with what was happening.

Qassem al-Nayyef was stretched out on the ground and Fatima was backed up against the wall, while, opposite her, a Jew in military dress was aiming his weapon. There was the smell of gunpowder, and Fatima calling for help, and the Jewish soldier, motionless, aiming his weapon—and Qassem al-Nayyef motionless on the ground, covered in blood.

As the soldier turned his gun on him, he felt no fear. Instead an instinct for survival awoke deep down inside him. His hand fell on the hilt of the dagger, and he pulled it out and raised his hand high.

The soldier looked at him fearfully, with a hint of fury too, then pulled the trigger. But there was no shot. He had no bullets left.

Abd al-Karim took a single, big leap, and the dagger came down on the soldier's chest. The rifle fell from the soldier's hand, and blood flowed out. The man swayed, then fell to the ground.

Chapter Six

From the account of Abd al-Rahman the Iraqi

Winter passed and the spring came. The sting went out of the cold and warmth started seeping back in.

In the last week of March there were several reorganizations among the battalions. Asad al-Shahba was transferred to the main headquarters at Jaba, while we stayed on at the camp not far from the town of Beisan. Najib had started yearning for his home town and he'd vowed to go there the first leave he got.

"It's odd," he said, "but all sorts of ordinary things become special when you're a long way from them."

Ahmad Bey was often away, and we hardly ever saw him but for the odd chance.

The fighting in Jaffa and Haifa, and in the Jerusalem and Hebron areas, was at its fiercest just then, and rumors and whispers were flying about that we were going to take part in a big offensive, which would be decisive for the fighting in the central region.

In our spare time we'd roam the nearby fields, meeting the peasants, sharing their barley bread and yogurt, and listening to their problems and worries and anxieties. Their fears had grown since the partition resolution and the date for the British withdrawal, and all the declarations from the Arab countries hadn't been able to calm them.

I spent my time writing letters to my mother, and to my friend Kazem, who was teaching at the Teacher's Institute in Baghdad, and I also wrote down some of my impressions and reflections and hid them in my suitcase.

Every so often Najib would come and find me writing, supposing I was writing to a woman. And no wonder either. In a wilderness like this, and in a situation like this one, a soldier feels all the more need for tenderness. Deep inside him, there's an insistent need for the other sex.

First it had been Asad al-Shahba, and now it was Najib's turn to be swept with a deep longing for his divorced wife Badriyyeh. The re-awakened love he felt for her had remorse mixed in with the yearning.

"If you love her so much," I asked once, when his longing wouldn't let him sleep, "then why did you divorce her?" He thought hard, then said:

"We didn't hate one another. Times were hard, that was all."

Which just goes to show how people try to search out some kind of reason when they don't have the courage to blame themselves.

Be that as it may, winter, as I said, was clearly over and spring had come. It had been a cruel winter, and we'd had to put up with bitter cold, poor food, a shortage of woolen clothing and scarcity of ammunition and equipment.

Ahmad Bey blamed the command in Damascus for not keeping their promises. Little by little we got used to all the postponements and learned to live with things being continually put off. We just had to be patient and put up with it.

Then, suddenly, Ahmad Bey came back from Jaba, where he'd been at a general meeting called by the Commander, and declared a state of alert. There was an unusual bustle in the camp now. Daily cleaning of weapons. Military cars examined. Oil and engines checked. Brakes tested. First aid kits checked. Then a day was fixed for target practice. Each soldier got to fire his rifle three times, and the artillery squad fired one 75-millimeter shell and one 105-millimeter shell. Then a convoy of trucks suddenly arrived with more ammunition, clothes and equipment.

"This is going to be the battle that decides things," Najib said one morning.

"Well," I said, "we've been waiting long enough."

After breakfast he started talking about his dream—the one he'd actually had in his sleep, I mean. It was about Badriyyeh, of course. In fact he'd told me about this particular dream many times, but with new things added each time. The new details were hopeful ones this time, lending the dream an air of joyful happiness.

"In my dream," he said, "I saw myself riding a winged mare, like al-Buraq, flying through the skies on her. I said: 'Blessed one, fly to Samakh.' And the blessed creature carried me across the mountains and valleys and plains.

"When the lake appeared, I laughed and the mare flapped her wings. I spoke to her again. 'Blessed one,' I said, 'put me down in front of Badriyyeh's house, so that I can see her but she can't see me.'

"So she swooped and put me down in front of the house of Badriyyeh's mother, Hajjeh Kulthoum. She was just performing the dawn prayer, and she had a blessed rosary of ninety-nine beads hanging around her neck. As for Badriyyeh, she was watering the flowerpots and drinking in the pure dawn air.

"I went up and called out: 'Badriyyeh! Badriyyeh, can you hear me?'

"She looked around, but she couldn't see me. She stopped in front of a green sapling planted at the front of the house. 'Badriyyeh,' I called. 'What are you doing?'

"She pointed to the sapling, and said: 'I'm watering this tree we call *muknissat al-janna.*' *

"I asked the blessed one to let Badriyyeh see me, but she answered: 'You can only make one wish at a time.'

"Then I called out: 'Badriyyeh, will you come back and be mine?' She didn't answer, but she put out her hand and caressed the leaves of the tree, filling the air with its sweet perfume. I woke up then, but how I wish I could have stayed in the dream longer."

Najib finished there, a kind of innocent joy radiating from him. He asked me if, from this safe distance, I'd write her a letter in his name. It should, he said, be eloquent and moving.

"Do you think she'll agree to come back to you?" I asked.

"Didn't I tell you?" Najib answered, smiling. "She caressed the leaves of the *muknissat al-janna*. That means she'll agree."

"But that was only a dream!" I said.

He reflected for a while, then said: "Well, anyway, I'll trust your way of writing."

I had to do something to bring joy to this man's heart, which passion had opened up so wide, so I grabbed the pen and started writing, beginning with the greeting and such. Then, suddenly, the air was filled with the sound of the siren calling us to alert.

The company gathered in the square in the center of the camp, and we all stood to attention. Ahmad Bey appeared and made a short speech, which he ended by announcing the company would move off, at zero hour, to area "A."

We went to finish our preparations, and Najib didn't dare broach the subject again; for there was a general feeling we were on the verge of a battle.

✖

---

* *Muknissat al-janna*: A decorative plant commonly set outside houses.

Zero hour.

The convoy moved out: trucks carrying soldiers, trucks carrying artillery, and the one armored car we possessed. I was sitting next to the driver in the front truck, while Najib was in a truck pulling a 75-millimeter gun.

It was midnight when we started off, and Ahmad Bey was in the small jeep at the head of the convoy, together with the guide who knew the way. I kept trying to guess where we were heading, but I couldn't be sure, although the scent from the orchards suggested we were moving up through some agricultural area. We didn't halt for a rest the way we'd done before. Finally, the driver told me we were moving toward the Ibn Amr plain.

At daybreak, as the sun's first rays were breaking through in the east, we were given the order to halt. We stopped at the bottom of a hill, in a thicket of wild trees, and spread out; and, since we'd been instructed to stay on alert, most of the soldiers slept in their uniforms. Tired out, I leaned my back against an oak tree and closed my eyes.

At noon we had a light snack of bread, tomatoes and *faqqous*,* in the shade of the green trees. We ate hungrily, and talked and drank water from our canteens. Then some of the soldiers, tempted by the warm air and the safety of the plains, made a circle for a *dabkeh*. Saber burst into song, singing to the nightingale perched on the pomegranate tree, and to Jafra who spread out her hair and wandered from orchard to orchard.

Najib was at the head of the dance circle, swaying his hips, and stamping his feet and jumping, while he sent his arm swirling in the air like a canary bird. A group of soldiers gathered around,

* *Faqqous*: A vegetable of the cucumber family.

clapping in time to the beat, and Saber, his love songs finished, started singing to the fire that burns on the mountain tops.

Then Ahmad Bey, who hadn't been with us, arrived suddenly, and spread gloom in place of the merriment by calling an immediate meeting of platoon leaders.

✖

I was appointed second-in-command to the platoon leader, and took part in the meeting, in which a plan was outlined to attack the settlement of Mishmar Ha-Emek, which the Jews called the "bastion of the plain."

It was to be a big operation, involving a battalion whose companies had been handpicked from all the other battalions. Our mission was to sabotage the secondary road leading to the settlement and block any reinforcements coming that way.

That evening the convoy set out once more, and we reached the village of Zarain in time for evening prayers. We were guests at the headquarters of Lieutenant-Colonel Muhammad al-Safa, where we were supplied with new weapons and equipment, and the villagers gave us a warm welcome. That same night we set off on foot toward our target.

We marched for hours until, finally, we reached the edge of the operational area, and the squads took up their positions along the different lines. I was in charge of the squad assigned to blow up the bridge linking this settlement with the other settlements in the north of the plain, while Najib commanded the squad that was to guard us and defend us against any sudden attack. We got everything ready, then just waited for zero hour, the time appointed for the general attack to begin.

The battle started at five in the evening. Our artillery all started shelling at once, from all directions, and the roar of the shells resounded in the skies. Our own company, with its various platoons and squads, carried out all the tasks assigned to it. We destroyed the bridge and took up a position to block any reinforcements that might arrive.

Ahmad Bey, who was in communication with headquarters, said:

"Commander Fawzi al-Kawuqji's commanding this battle in person."

As the battle got under way, an assault force advanced on the outposts of the settlement supported by artillery and armored cars. The attacking infantrymen reached the barbed wire and started cutting it, while the cars sent out a fierce bombardment.

A stream of shots was fired at our troops from the towers, and the infantry flung back a hail of hand grenades. Then the armored cars approached, and the outposts and towers both fell silent. After two hours the battle was still raging.

As night fell it started raining, and the commander halted the attack, ordering the forces to retreat to the hills. Then he sent a warning to the settlement, demanding that its leaders surrender and send a delegation to see him.

After a little while it stopped raining—it had just been a light spring shower. Najib came up, with his head wrapped in a *kaffiyyeh* and a sten gun in his hand. He was delighted with the gun, which he'd acquired at Zarain.

"I'd hoped I could be part of the attacking force," he said, and he wasn't lying either. The air was full of the scents of spring, all the more so after the rains.

"We took part in the battle," I said. "That's the main thing."

There was a brief period of silence, spoiled only by the crackling of the wireless as a soldier attending Ahmad Bey fiddled with it.

"Why did the commander halt the attack?" Najib asked.

"That's all part of the plan," I said.

I don't know what made him think, at that moment, of our other comrade, but suddenly he said:

"Where do you think Asad al-Shahba is now?"

I tried to think. He'd been chosen by Lieutenant-Colonel al-Safa to be one of a group guarding the commander himself. He'd been sent to Toubas first, and from there on to Qabatiyyeh, and then on to Jaba. He must be in al-Mansi now, at the center of operations.

"God willing," I said, "we'll see him after we've won."

After a while the soldier manning the wireless shut it down, and there was silence. Some of us slept, while others took turns at sentry duty.

Next day the news spread of a message from the settlement to the commander, that a delegation from the settlement would come for negotiations that afternoon. The watchword from Ahmad Bey was "vigilance and caution."

It was a sunny day, and people came hurrying over from the surrounding villages to help us out. The day passed without a single shot being fired. The silence was uncanny—it hardly seemed possible that a whole front of a few square miles could stay quiet without the whizzing of bullets or the roaring of cannons.

In the afternoon Ahmad Bey visited all the positions, including ours. He told us the delegation from the settlement had arrived at the headquarters of Lieutenant-Colonel Mahdi Saleh, made up of all the important people from the settlement accompanied by a colonel of the British army. The delegation had asked for a 24-hour truce to bury the dead and transport the wounded for treatment.

Ahmad Bey fell suddenly silent, putting his head in his hands with an air of utter despondency. He sat there with us on the soft grass, waiting, like us, for the outcome; and the soldiers, looking at him, caught his mood, wondering why he was so gloomy.

Najib shot me a questioning look, and I motioned to him to say nothing. We had to be patient at times like this. As the silence lingered, the soldiers started to drift away again, including Najib, who went off to find something to do.

Ahmad Bey raised his head. His face was flushed and his eyes bloodshot. His gaze fell on me, and he muttered, as though to himself:

"He shouldn't have given them a long truce like that. He shouldn't have done it."

Then he got up and strode rapidly away, as though he was fleeing from himself.

Within the hour he was back with our platoon commander, calm now, his face clear, and he told us our platoon was to move on to the village of al-Mansi where we'd be told what we were to do. Then he left, shaking each individual man by the hand, and wishing us luck and success, in the sad, breaking voice of someone talking to his children.

We didn't understand the reason for this sudden show of emotion, but, as we set off, we were moved in our turn. For the first time we felt a kind of compassion for this man who'd perplexed us for so long.

In the truck, Najib said:

"I remember his face when he came back from the battle of al-Ziraa. That's just how he looked then. Slaughtered sheep," he added, "laugh at sheep who've been skinned."

Talk turned away from Ahmad Bey then, as we started thinking about our mission.

We reached al-Mansi just as it was getting dark, and were assigned sleeping quarters in various houses attached to the headquarters. The village was in total darkness, because a blackout had been imposed as a precaution. A young officer was waiting for us, and he gave orders for us to be provided with a meal, then told us to rest until next morning, when the commander would address us in person.

Most of the soldiers went to bed early, but Najib and I went out into the small square for a breath of fresh air, and to be somewhere that wasn't quite so dark. The young officer was out there as well, walking with his arms behind his back. Perhaps he was tired of the silence and darkness too.

When he caught up with us, he stopped and smiled, and we had a talk with him, trying to find out what it was like at the front lines. But he wasn't giving anything away. He sounded anxious, though, and that gave us an inkling of how difficult and complicated the situation was. He made an effort to change the subject.

"You're lucky," he said jokingly. "You're sleeping in Colonel Nour al-Din's quarters."

We went back to our quarters and stretched out on the mattresses that had been hurriedly put out for us. Then I closed my eyes.

When we woke in the morning, light was filtering in through the open window, to reveal a small but neat room. In the corner was a table with shaving gear laid out on it, along with an empty vase and a small notebook with a pen on the top. Hanging on one wall was a military uniform with stars at the shoulders and a medal pinned on the front—Colonel Nour al-Din's presumably. On the wall opposite hung a navy-blue vest—sleeveless, puffed out—with big pockets.

Najib was staring at it, rubbing his eyes.

"It's the same one!" he said. "The navy-blue vest. The bullet-proof vest." He leaped up. "Don't you remember I told you about it? I swear it's the same one!"

I remembered well enough. I didn't, though, share my friend Najib's amazement. The vest had simply been passed on, from one officer to the next, until at last it had reached Colonel Nour al-Din.

Najib was firing questions, obviously intent on stirring up a hornet's nest. I left him and went out into the courtyard, where our comrades were washing and shaving.

Hot tea came, along with bread and yellow cheese, and we all ate; all except Najib, who stayed on in the room so long I thought he might be taking the vest down and putting it on.

As it happened the commanding officer didn't come and see us that night, and nor did any of his aides. All we saw was a simple non-commissioned officer, who came with a big truck to transfer us to a large-scale barracks.

At the entrance to the camp we were met by Captain Ma'moun al-Bitar, who had a big, confident smile on his face and greeted us one by one. Then, being a friendly kind of officer, he followed us into our big tent and sat down with us. At noon he had lunch with us, then gave us a few details of the mission we'd soon be embarking on, which involved supporting the troops who were fighting at the gates of Jerusalem, under the command of Abd al-Qader al-Husseini.

He was full of confidence, and we loved him from the first, feeling not just secure but fired with enthusiasm. When, we wondered impatiently, would we be setting off for the holy city?

The road to Jerusalem was long—long and winding. We passed through plains and lowlands, plowed our way along dirt roads and across farm lands. Our convoy passed among peasant houses, where we'd catch the smell of bread baking in the ovens, and we'd slow down when flocks of sheep crossed in front of us. Most of the time we were traveling along a road flanked by oak trees or cactus plants. I couldn't stop thinking of the approaching battle, imagining a whole horizon on fire.

A little way off from Jerusalem, we stopped at an olive grove by the roadside for a meal and a rest. Captain Ma'moun sat with us, eating what we were eating and chatting with us.

He spread a sense of optimism, inspiring us to courage and resolve, filling us with pleasure at the thought of playing our part in defending the holy city.

He spoke with an elegant Damascene accent, and never took off the glasses that made him look even more handsome and made his Damascene complexion seem fairer still.

"I'm starting to believe in him," Najib said, as we went back to our trucks and the convoy moved on again. He took a drink from his flask, then muttered: "When are we going to reach Jerusalem?"

We got there at last—or, strictly speaking, to the gateway of Jerusalem, where a deputation from al-Husseini's forces was waiting for us at the foot of a hill overlooking the holy city. We clambered down to rest while they met with Captain Ma'moun and the non-commissioned officers. The atmosphere, I noticed, was heavy, and their faces were dark, reflecting some dreadful event.

As the meeting went on, Najib came to ask me what was going on, and I just stood there anxiously, not knowing how to answer. Then Captain Ma'moun came back, his face flushed and morose. The soldiers, no doubt noticing the hard lines etched on it, gathered around him.

"Brothers," he said. "We came here to the aid of al-Qastel, but it seems we've arrived too late."

The words fell like daggers, and everyone looked dazed. Captain Ma'moun whipped off his glasses to reveal the tears falling from his honey-colored eyes.

"We've lost al-Qastel," he said in a low voice. "And we've lost the fighter Abd al-Qader al-Husseini."

A tremor passed through the assembled men, along with a sense of searing pain. Najib went up to the captain.

"Sir," he said. "We must do something. We can't just go back defeated."

Captain Ma'moun put his glasses back on, remembering, maybe, that he had to stay calm and set an example. But Najib's words had cut through the dejected silence. From the rear came the cry: "God is great!" Then the cry was taken up by everyone, echoing on all sides: "God is great!"

Captain Ma'moun turned away, and the non-commissioned officer ordered us to spread out in the olive grove and wait for further orders. Then the command came for the artillery platoon to move to the front lines and shell Jewish positions in the western half of the city.

Next morning Captain Ma'moun told us we were to go back to our old positions that afternoon and play our part in the battle of Mishmar Ha-Emek, which was still raging fiercely. We were split into two groups, and a feeling of confusion crept into our minds even before it entered the ranks. Najib was furiously angry.

"Don't wait for me," he said, passing straight by me. "I'm going off there."

He didn't say where "there" was, but it could only mean he was staying on in Jerusalem, staying with those who were defending the city. There wasn't any way I could talk him out of it, and he certainly wasn't in the mood to ask for my approval. He just said it and went off. I gazed at him as he walked through the olive grove with his rifle, leaped over a wall and disappeared. It was a special kind of sorrow, I think, that gripped me then—a sorrow more like a lament than anything else.

And so, that afternoon, we started back to our positions, to take our part in the battle of Mishmar Ha-Emek. Captain Ma'moun, serious-faced, stood there in his dark glasses and made a moving and eloquent speech, designed to raise our morale, until our eyes filled with tears. The battle at Mishmar Ha-Emek, he said, was hanging in the balance. The enemy had taken advantage of the truce to bring in more Hagannah forces and the position of our own troops in Marj Ibn Amr was precarious.

Everyone was moved, and, slowly, a wave of enthusiasm swept the ranks. Someone cried out: "God is great!" Then everyone took up the shout. We climbed onto the trucks, and, as we drove off, the fields set out with us. So did the olive trees, and the prickly pears, and the china trees.

Saber's voice rose from the heart of the convoy, singing to the lightning that flashes beyond the mountains and the thunder that rolls down from the peaks. The men joined in the chorus, and we grew ever more uplifted as the cars gathered speed. We hardly felt the time passing, and, by the time we reached Marj Ibn Amr, we were all burning to join the battle.

We went to regional headquarters for a short rest. Then Captain Ma'moun received a telegram from the commander-in-chief and called us around.

"Brothers," he cried. "The battle at Mishmar Ha-Emek's getting bigger. The enemy's brought in more reinforcements, and we're to help block the offensive."

And so we did, countering the Hagannah troops who'd attacked us on a broad front. Most of our men had been forced to retreat in face of an onslaught by forces superior in numbers and equipment. We helped break the encirclement around an artillery corps that was on the point of being captured, throwing ourselves into the rescue and, after a fierce struggle, pulling the corps out. But Captain Ma'moun, who was leading the charge, was hit by a bullet and fell. Finally the battle subsided and our forces returned to their old positions, the spirit of the martyr Captain Ma'moun still fluttering over us like a green bird.* Even though he was gone, we still felt him there, alive, with us, and we recounted stories about his courage, about his character and simplicity. The commander-in-chief

---

* *Green bird*: One of the birds of paradise and symbolically associated with martyrs.

selected a few men, including Asad al-Shahba, to escort his body to Damascus.

It had been a strange battle, a battle full of breaches, ending with our withdrawal and nothing gained at all. I was promoted, becoming a platoon leader; yet I was beset by feelings of bitterness and rancor, of humiliation even.

We went back to our position, on the outskirts of al-Mansi. Colonel Nour al-Din's uniform was still hanging on the wall in the room there, but the vest had disappeared. I remembered Najib, who'd said goodbye to me and gone off.

May God's blessing be with that brave man, I thought, wherever he goes. May his dreams be filled with deer and butterflies and flowers; with the scent of the trees of *muknissat al-janna,* and with the smell of his beloved, who inspired his heart with such undying passion.

Chapter Seven

Radi opened his eyes at the first crow of the rooster. The bed was warm and a delightful sense of languor possessed him. It was so pleasant, so comfortable, sleeping there in the reception room amidst all the pillows and cushions and copper pots.

Poking his head out, he saw his uncle was still fast asleep, breathing peacefully. Still he lay there, listening to the crowing of the roosters who were each trying to outdo the other. He could tell the difference between the crows of his family's roosters and the crowing of his uncle's, which had been brought there after the dreadful event.

He looked toward the window. It was still dark outside, but, though dawn was some way off, the smell of the firewood in the ovens was spreading. He stayed there, still wrapped in warmth and languor. Many things had changed since that ill-fated night, whose marks were still etched in his uncle's face. His uncle had started viewing the world differently now.

He heard the creaking of the front gate, then his father's voice calling out to the Creator of all beings, the Grantor of fortune;

this was his daily custom, just like the morning cup of coffee. He was always the first to wake in the house, and he'd open the door to greet the coming day, celebrating the dawn in his own way. He'd perform his ablutions and pray, drink tea and coffee, then get on his horse and ride off to check his fields and property.

Next he'd rouse Khaled al-Zaher, who slept in the small room next to the stable and usually woke the moment he heard the bolt creak in the big gate, racing off to prepare the water for the Haj's ablutions and put out feed for the horses. It was his job to feed the carriage horse and Haj Hussein's mare, along, now, with Abd al-Karim's mare, which was the only one of its kind in Samakh.

After this came the voice of Ahmad al-Mulla, who always knocked but didn't wait for permission to enter. He was carrying the pure water he'd brought from the furthest point of the lake he could reach, and he'd pour it out into the big clay pot, splashing the dog Wolf, who'd rouse himself and start sniffing here and there, poking his head into the reception room but not daring to enter. Life was stirring in the house, the light was spreading, and al-Zabadneh's voice rose high from the minaret, filling the dewy dawn.

Radi opened his eyes once more, hearing Fatima's footsteps as she came down the staircase from the attic. She'd been sleeping there ever since the events of that tragic night, when her husband Qassem al-Nayyef had been killed. She'd come down wrapped right up in black, and she'd put out feed for the chickens, then milk the brindled cow before it was let loose to pasture with the calves. Then came Radi's mother, who went out into the courtyard and lit the oven, letting it heat up while she put water on the pots of *utrah*, sending a sweet fragrance spreading around.

His uncle stirred in his bed, waking up now, and Radi, realizing he'd have to get up, tossed his coverings aside. His father came in, his shirtsleeves rolled up ready for prayer, and wished them good morning, upon which his uncle Abd al-Karim got up himself and went to wash in the barn.

Radi rose and went out into the courtyard, where the fire in the oven was burning well and the dough for the bread was ready and waiting. Fatima, having finished feeding the chickens, emerged from the barn carrying a basin full of milk.

His mother had always been fond of Fatima, but ever since the tragedy she'd surpassed herself in caring for her. Two weeks had passed now since the terrible night, but the tears hadn't dried in Fatima's eyes. She rarely talked about it unless someone brought it up, and his mother never left her by herself except when she slept.

Every so often she'd bump into Abd al-Karim in the courtyard, and he'd ask: "How are you, Fatima?" Then the tears would roll down her cheeks. "I'm alright, Uncle, thank God," she'd say.

Sorrow had made its home in her eyelids, and in her black dress and drawn-out silences. Yet the moment she raised her eyes to gaze through the window at the horizon, her handsome face would re-appear, brushed over by a noble sorrow; her eyes held a special magic, and she appeared beautiful for all her pain.

She worked very conscientiously in this new house she'd moved to. She still fed the chickens and attended to the brindled cow, feeding it and giving it water to drink, cleaning it and wiping its brow with affection and tenderness.

Here she was now, carrying the milk pan and setting it down by the fire, cutting up the dough and shaping it into loaves. Abd al-Karim came out in his white sleeping gown, said good morning to everyone in the courtyard and went into the reception room, where the Haj had almost finished his prayers. Abd al-Karim changed into his street clothes, into the new *qimbaz** which he took out of the suitcase laid down in the corner, taking out, too, a white voile headdress which he put on over his head, on top of the black braids. Then he put on his belt, placing the silver dagger in the middle of it.

* *Qimbaz*: A long, straight robe, closed at the sides.

That was a sign he was going on a journey.

"Where are you off to, Abd al-Karim?" the Haj asked, when he'd finished his prayers. There was an eagerness in his tone, for he'd begun treating him differently since the recent events.

Abd al-Karim didn't answer. He'd just decided to go on a trip, that was all. Perhaps he was tired of all the questions, the endless chatter, the same repeated conversations.

He'd told everybody, there in the reception room, of the events of that terrible night, when he'd stabbed the soldier in the chest with his dagger—the night Qassem al-Nayyef had been shot. Still, though, people just wouldn't stop asking questions.

"Where are you going, Uncle?" Radi asked.

"I'm going to fulfill a vow."

Those were his words. But where was he going? He wouldn't say, keeping his sudden departure wrapped in a mantle of mystery. He'd said nothing about the trip the night before. The reception room had been chock full of guests drawn by their curiosity, and Abd al-Karim had answered all their queries; he'd been blessed with a patience that allowed him to go on recounting the story, and telling how he'd taken the soldier's weapon after he'd killed him. He refused to tell anyone what kind of weapon it was because, along with some grenades and a pouch, it had become the property of the National Committee. All he'd say was that it was a quick-firing gun.

He told how God had granted him strength and planted courage in his heart, for what boldness had made him, Abd al-Karim, stab the soldier, when all his life he'd never so much as killed a chicken?

"Be careful, Abd al-Karim," he was told. "There's a war out there. The whole country's in a ferment. It's not safe to travel."

Suddenly Fatima appeared, standing in the doorway in her black dress, with her face that had grown paler now, her hair wrapped in a black cover. She stood there without a word, having caught some of the conversation perhaps. Behind her, in her turn, Umm* Radi looked in.

"Why are you looking at me like that?" Abd al-Karim asked.

"Where are you off to, Uncle?" Fatima said, beginning to weep. "Don't we have enough troubles already?"

It seemed as if Abd al-Karim was weakening and might change his mind. Then he got a grip on himself and tried to change the atmosphere.

"God is One," he said. "Where's breakfast? Where's breakfast, Fatima, eh?"

It was the first time, since that dreadful night, that he'd addressed her in such an intimate way, and it gave everyone the impression things were returning to normal. A ghost of a smile passed over her face, unnoticed almost because of the tear rolling down her round cheek and onto her chin. Umm Radi broke into a smile, while Fatima wiped her face and Haj Hussein breathed a deep sigh of relief. As for Abd al-Karim, he sat down on the cushions, giving no sign of whether or not he was still intent on his journey.

In a short time the breakfast table was ready, and the Haj insisted the two women should share the food with them. It was probably the first time such a thing had ever happened in Haj Hussein's reception room—for two women eating from the same dishes as the men.

Radi gazed at Fatima, who was beginning to look better, drawn out of her sorrows, while his father talked easily, making the atmosphere still more relaxed by his consideration and kindness. From time to time a smile passed their lips, the first since that dreadful night.

---

* *Umm*: Mother or mother of. Women in many Arab countries are called by the name of their first-born child, the first male child having ascendancy. Thus Khadijeh is also called "Umm Radi."

Abd al-Karim, looking very smart in his travel clothes and wearing the dagger at his side, was the center of attention. Suddenly they heard the horn of the yellow car—Abd al-Karim must have arranged for Hamid Abu Hamid to come.

It was a shock, and there was a sense of dejection, the happy atmosphere threatening to turn to gloom. But Abd al-Karim got right up and hurried out, wearing a light pair of slippers, and in a little while he was back.

"Don't worry," he said, without further ado. "I've canceled the trip."

Their faces relaxed once more, and Umm Radi felt emboldened to say to her husband:

"I wish you'd take us with you to the Duwair estate today."

Without this special atmosphere she would never have dared address him like that in front of other people. The Haj reflected.

"Very well," he said. "Go and get ready. We'll leave in an hour."

Umm Radi looked at Fatima, who turned away, her brow darkened.

"We'll visit Hafiza," Umm Radi whispered, "and come back in the evening."

"I'll come with you, Haj," Abd al-Karim broke in. "I feel heavy. I want to get some fresh air."

Radi got up, not waiting to hear all the attempts to get Fatima to go with them. He hurried off to tell Khaled al-Zaher, who, pleased at the news, went to get everything ready and saddle the mares. As for Wolf, who was always quick to sense something was happening, he started pouncing on Radi's feet and generally behaving like a silly puppy.

✖

The carriage set off in the first morning sun, with Radi and Khaled al-Zaher riding in front, while Umm Radi and Fatima sat in the carriage on cushions specially put there for them, along with the baby, Maher. The brindled milk cow was also tethered at the back, for Fatima had insisted on taking her along. Wolf had been left behind to guard the house, left howling behind the closed gates despite all his vain efforts to go along with them.

The carriage set off slowly, while the two men, Haj Hussein and Abd al-Karim, each giving rein to his mare, raced away. Sometimes they'd gallop, at other times they'd trot alongside one another and talk.

The carriage passed by the side of the lake. The road to the estate overlooked it, so that wherever you were you could see the lake mirrored back. The water was an intense blue color, and migrating white birds were flying over it, while there, on the depths of the lake, was a boat traveling further out.

On the shore a fisherman was guiding a kayak, already seeking his livelihood so early in the morning, while Ahmad al-Mulla stood on the pier, his equipment laid by his side as he took a moment off to reflect.

"This lake's like the sun," Umm Radi said. "It's the giver of life."

Fatima swept the calm blue waters with her gaze, but felt no lightening of the spirit, felt nothing moving inside her. In vain Umm Radi tried to draw her out from her sorrow.

The estate came into view. You could see the crops now, the ears of corn upright in the sun. There were peasants dotted about everywhere. The hillside was filled with tents. The cattle were in their pastures, and the carriage passed flocks of black and white sheep whose shepherds were sitting under the shady trees, while landowners rode about on their horses checking everything out, and Hafiza—who they called "the sister of men"—was standing waiting at the entrance to the black tent.

The two men had already arrived and turned their horses over to the herdsmen. They were lying on some bedding and cushions in the part of the tent assigned for the men, while Hafiza's husband was offering them bitter coffee, the only thing he could make out there in the wild.

The carriage arrived, and was greeted by Hafiza, who kissed Radi and his mother and hugged Fatima, each weeping on the other's shoulder. Hafiza, though, quickly wiped her eyes and drew herself erect. She was dressed in a black peasant gown, with a cloth belt around her midriff and what looked like army boots on her feet. She pulled herself together and took the baby, Maher, from his mother's arms, cuddling and kissing him. Then she motioned the women into their part of the tent.

A lot of bustle and merriment was going on everywhere, and Radi went about, looking constantly to see what was happening. The shepherds slaughtered a fat sheep, cut it into pieces and started cooking it. Meanwhile the aunt kept trying to console Fatima. Then large numbers of women milking and making butter came to join the group. While the men played games of *sija* and *minqala,** Hafiza took the women to watch the sheep being sheared, then on to the milking shed, and from there to the pen for newly delivered calves, who competed with the milkers to get their mothers' milk.

✖

Fatima scanned the pasture, searching for her brindled cow, but couldn't see any trace of it. That disturbed her and made her nervous, but before she could say anything Hafiza pulled her into the tent for lunch.

An invigorating spring breeze blew up, and after lunch Haj

* *Sija, minqala*: Wooden board games, somewhat similar in principle to checkers.

Hussein stretched out and tried to take a nap, while Abd al-Karim went for a walk with Radi, who listened eagerly to his uncle's conversations with the men.

By the afternoon the women had finished washing up, and they'd run out of stories and news, and gossiped about everyone they could possibly think of. Fatima was still searching for her brindled cow, and finally, unable to bear it any longer, asked Khaled al-Zaher to go and look for it over the wide plain.

✖

At that moment a horseman, riding an unsaddled horse and carrying a hunting rifle in his hand, galloped by. He stopped to exchange some words with the shepherds, then spurred his horse and galloped on. He'd come from Tallat al-Qaser, and was hunting down a highly dangerous rabid dog, who had killed great numbers of sheep there and, having been chased off, had been seen heading toward Tallat al-Duwair. He'd warned the shepherds to be on the alert, telling them he was determined to hunt the dog down.

The news spread quickly, and the atmosphere changed, with everybody worried. The shepherds started rounding up the herds of cattle and flocks of sheep.

Even Aunt Hafiza, the sister of men, who was responsible for everyone, got agitated and, after apologizing to the women, started issuing orders to everyone around her. Even her husband, who had no clear function there, didn't escape.

Haj Hussein woke to find an atmosphere of panic and thought for a moment there was a Jewish attack on the estate. When he learned of the rabid dog, he too became anxious and preoccupied. Abd al-Karim, though, advised people not to spread panic. It would be better, he said, to join in hunting down the animal rather than hanging around. Meanwhile Radi watched two rams butting one another with their horns.

Fatima came back panting.

"The cow's missing, Uncle," she said. "It's missing!"

Abd al-Karim, reading some premonition of disaster in her face, said to himself: "There is no power or strength except in God."

Then, from the edge of the field, Khaled al-Zaher came running for all he was worth, like a whirlwind, and once more Abd al-Karim felt that what was destined had come to pass. He felt no surprise when Khaled al-Zaher panted:

"The cow's been bitten by the rabid dog. She's over there by the edge of the river. She's dying."

Fatima cried out and started beating her cheeks. The rams stopped fighting, and Radi didn't know what to do. Abd al-Karim leaped onto his horse and galloped toward the river, followed by Haj Hussein. They crossed the whole expanse of the field, then down to the bank. There, between the oleander trees, was the stricken cow, blood oozing from different parts of its body, its mouth and nose covered in foam. It was trembling, unable to stand any longer. It had been mangled mercilessly by the dog, and evidently lain there suffering for some time. As the men approached, it gave a last convulsion, then its eyes stood out and it stopped moving. Abd al-Karim was filled with distress and he turned away to fight off a sudden urge to weep.

Haj Hussein laid a hand on his shoulder.

"Come on," he said.

They went back, dejected. Abd al-Karim's head was bowed, feeling these things were all omens of misfortune, of a misfortune, above all, that still lay concealed in the future. Haj Hussein felt anxious too, filled with foreboding, thinking of what lay ahead: the coming days and an unknown disaster dropping down from on high.

✖

As the carriage returned with its passengers that evening, a cold wind blew, sending a chill through their bodies. Khaled al-Zaher drove, with Radi silent alongside him, while Umm Radi suckled the baby, Maher, and Fatima's face was suddenly full of wrinkles. She looked very old. The two men rode behind, dispirited. It was as though the wind was drawing them back.

Chapter Eight

Another omen of misfortune came. Abd al-Karim al-Hamad was racing the wind on the back of his white mare, whose noble neck was covered by a golden mane; and this horse, with all its ornate accoutrements, whose hooves hardly touched the ground between al-Hammeh and Samakh, stumbled suddenly and fell.

Abd al-Karim was sent flying through the air, as the mare rolled over the pitted, stony ground. Then he staggered to his feet. The mare too got up for a moment, then dropped back on the ground, the agony showing in her eyes. She'd broken one of her legs and couldn't walk, or even stand.

Abd al-Karim braced himself to approach the animal, wiping her forehead and passing his hand across the forelock and mane. Then he patted the rump. Still the mare didn't rise, but sprawled, whinnying, still more onto her side. Her right foreleg was broken between the knee and the hoof, and with that Abd al-Karim's heart broke too. The pains were increasing, the sorrows multiplying. This misfortune had come right out of the blue.

He was there, alone, in a vast, desolate wilderness. He gazed at his noble mare, unable to believe what had happened. A sense of misfortune pursued him. Was there some disaster about to strike? Why were all these omens falling just on him?

He passed his hand again over the brow of the patient horse, who, at that moment, must have been suffering agonies of pain. As he caressed the brow and mane, she tried again, repeatedly, to rise, but finally surrendered to the ground strewn with pebbles and thorns.

Abd al-Karim unfastened the heavy, ornate saddle and lifted it from the horse's back, and, as he did so, it was as though a knife were piercing between his ribs. He'd been hurt in the fall too, he realized now, and it would be more painful still when the injury was no longer fresh.

He took off the saddlebag with its colored fringes and copper stirrup, then unfastened the reins and the woolen halter, leaving the horse free of any encumbrance. Suddenly he saw tears shining in the beast's eyes. It didn't seem like an animal at that moment; it had the eyes of a human, rather, the look of a child in pain. He gazed around, into the silence, seeing just an abandoned rail track.

What was he to do? Samakh was still some way off, and so was the road people used. He thought of leaving the horse and going to try and find help of some sort. He knew well enough, though, what they did to a thoroughbred with one of its legs broken. One bullet from a hunting rifle, and that would be it.

The force of the disaster struck him. The mare had the same look as the brindled cow, before it died there by the river bank.

Life's worn you right down, Abd al-Karim, he thought. What is there left?

He bent down and took hold of the halter hanging down from her head, the fringed halter braided with colored wool, took a few steps with it, then turned again. He could hear the noise of the horse, the panting and whinnying. Should he go and leave her there?

She might get thirsty or hungry. No, she'd grazed just an hour before in the pastures. You could still see the bits of grass on her hooves. He could set off before it got dark. And so he left her there, leaving with her the saddle and reins and spurs, groaning in his frustration.

✖

After a lot of walking he came across a shepherd riding a mule along the road from Umm al-Masari to Samakh, and the man took him up and dropped him near al-Karantina. As soon as he dismounted, a sharp pain began tearing at his chest. He could feel it in his right ribs. Now the wound wasn't fresh any longer, and he could tell he had broken ribs, or at best severe bruising. The shepherd went off, anxious to reach his destination before nightfall.

Abd al-Karim gritted his teeth, his hand still firmly closed around the halter that had gone around the mare's head. He was having trouble walking, every step bringing him a shooting pain from the depths of his chest. It was sunset now, and the road between al-Karantina and Samakh was deserted. Nothing but telephone poles and the barking of distant dogs.

Still he walked on, in spite of everything. Feeling, after a while, that his grip on the halter was loosening, that he might drop it, he steeled himself, increasing his efforts to hold on.

The pain bearing down on his chest was remorseless now. He had to fight not to cry out, and when he couldn't walk any more, he sat down on the ground, huddled up, keeping tight hold of the halter as though he wanted to put an end to something unbearable. Still, though, there was no let up in the pain.

Everywhere had grown dark now. He made an effort, pulled himself together, and started walking again, then, suddenly, quickened his stride. A breeze blew up and, through all his pain, he remembered the white mare lying, alone and abandoned, on the dirt road.

Here it was again, this obscure thing pursuing him. Curses, hyenas, Jews, rabid dogs, ditches. What would be next?

Soon he found the intense pain beginning to drag him down. The sharp point of the pain, he realized, was piercing the calm surface of his forbearance; and he felt, too, a great wave of howling and crying and lamentation, pressing inside his head, making his head burst almost. How did he go on, walking on hot coals?

On the outskirts of the small town, he finally dropped in a faint, and passers-by picked him up.

✖

When he opened his eyes, he found himself in a bed surrounded by a number of men he didn't recognize at first. They were talking together, but stopped the moment he showed a sign of movement.

"He's all right," he heard one man say.

"He's opening his eyes," another said.

"Ask him if he can talk," said a third voice.

He felt like turning away and plunging back into sleep, but the pain had returned, though it was less sharp than before. They rubbed his forehead and his eyes. Then, when he tried to move to a more comfortable position, the needle-sharp pain shot through his chest once more; and when they tried to help him, he screamed from an agony that gored him like a raging bull.

As the men fell back, the face of Haj Hussein appeared. So he was there with his brother-in-law. Haj Hussein pressed his hand encouragingly, and asked:

"Can you talk, Abd al-Karim?"

He nodded, making a vain attempt to open his mouth. Radi's face came into view, and Abd al-Karim's eyes filled with tears. He tried once more to talk, and, this time, managed some disjointed words.

He was talking, but didn't know what he was saying.

Then there was a commotion, and heated discussion. Some people went off and others came.

Abd al-Karim found himself in the hands of several men. They stripped off his clothes and one of them started pressing down on his chest. Once more the raging bull was impaling him on its horns, lifting him up, then tossing him down to the ground. He screamed, crying out for help, then fell silent.

When, many hours later, he opened his eyes, there was a cast around his chest and the bonesetter was standing nearby, waiting.

"How are you feeling now, Abd al-Karim?" he asked.

Now? He could hear well enough, and he could talk too. He was aware, now, that he was sleeping on a bed in the house of his brother-in-law, Haj Hussein. He could see and hear and smell.

"I'm all right, thank God," he said.

With that the bonesetter went to open the door, and Umm Radi and Fatima entered, their faces drawn and their eyes red from too much weeping.

"Why have you been crying so much?" he asked. "Did I die and come back to life again?"

The bonesetter gestured to them to say nothing. Umm Radi sat on the edge of the bed, while Fatima stayed standing. He met their eyes and made an effort to smile. It was as though he'd come back after being away for years.

"Thank God you're all right, Abd al-Karim," Umm Radi said, pressing his hand.

He wanted to talk now. He'd been treated, he realized, in the traditional Arab way, his broken bones reset.

"Where's Radi?" he asked.

"He went with them," she said.

He knew straight away what that meant, knew well enough where they'd gone. His eyes fell on the halter lying in a corner of the room, and he didn't feel like talking after all.

Fatima approached, the very picture of sorrow.

"Get better soon, Uncle," she said.

He was astounded at the sight of her face, with all its wrinkles.

"I'm all right, Fatima," he said, trying to console her.

He closed his eyes, and a powerful urge to sleep swept over him. Umm Radi got off the bed and motioned to Fatima to leave the room with her.

✖

The men came back some time after midnight, hungry and weary. They got down from their horses and came in through the wide gate that had stayed open since nightfall.

There was confusion and clamor. Khaled al-Zaher lit the lanterns and woke the people of the house. The ovens were lit once more, and the smoke spread. Soon fresh hot bread emerged from the *taboun* oven, and the food was taken from the pots and eaten, though the men all had a lump in their throats. As they ate they lived once more through the events of the night.

Haj Hussein felt the need for company tonight, to banish feelings of loneliness. He greeted the men, and welcomed them. One man becomes many through his brothers.

Radi crept to the attic and put his ear to the door, thinking that he might know, from a sigh or a movement, whether his uncle was asleep or awake. He thought for a moment of knocking at the door, but held back. Tonight, he knew, his uncle had suffered agonizing pain, and was now too deeply asleep to be woken even by the din around them.

✖

Radi had been with them when they set off toward al-Hammeh, to a point not far from the settlement of Shaar Ha-Golan, where the mare with the broken leg was suffering so cruelly in silence. They spread out in the moonlight, searching for her over the plain, and found her soon enough, with the saddle, stirrup, reins and saddlebag alongside.

Muhammad al-Jafil got down from his horse and approached the mare. He was a horse expert, as well as a cupper, bonesetter and herbal healer, and he carried out circumcisions too. He bent over her to examine her, the mare resisting weakly as the men helped him lift her.

Muhammad al-Jafil examined the leg, then looked up.

"It's no use," he said.

There was no more to say. The men remounted their horses and rode back home, leaving Muhammad al-Jafil to fire the merciful bullet into the broken mare. They preferred not to watch, getting up on their horses as though fleeing from themselves, leaving Muhammad al-Jafil to shoot her between her eyes with his hunting rifle.

Radi climbed down the attic stairs, went back to the reception room and sat silently among the men. When, at last, they'd left, and the last part of the night was filled with silence, Haj Hussein said:

"Why don't you go to bed, son?"

"I don't feel like sleeping," Radi answered briefly. His father, he knew, couldn't sleep either.

Realizing, perhaps, that his son had started understanding things, and suffering from them, Haj Hussein didn't rebuke his son. Instead he said gently:

"Then you can sit here with me until it's time for the dawn prayers. We'll go and pray, then sleep until morning."

Radi liked the idea of this, and he smiled and nodded. Everything was silent and dark. Khaled al-Zaher, tired out, was asleep.

"Have you been to see how your uncle is?" Haj Hussein asked.

"He's asleep," Radi said. "He's been fast asleep ever since the bonesetter left."

Neither of them said anything after that. The silence stretched on, the father almost able to see the ideas his son was turning over in his mind. And the son, too, understood what was going through his father's mind. He listened intently, sensing the agitation, like the din of the sea ferry, churning in the depths of this steadfast old man.

Chapter Nine

Ominous events spread to the whole small town now. At dawn, fierce fighting started in Tiberias, explosions rocking the town and echoing as far as Samakh. People went up onto their rooftops and down to the shore, while Mansour got up onto the roof of the station to watch events through his binoculars. When Hamid Abu Hamid, down below, asked him what he could see, he just said:

"Fires, burning all over the place."

Not satisfied, Hamid Abu Hamid got into his car and raced along to the road that led to the Bab al-Toum bridge, where the Jordan River left the lake after passing right through it from north to south. There he stood by the huts of the fishermen, who hadn't gone out fishing today. Abu Abd Allah, the oldest of them, was sitting near his boat at the back of a tin shack, surrounded by some of his men who were drinking tea and waiting.

What were they waiting for? Nothing really—or maybe for the unknown. Waiting for more misfortunes and disasters. The waters of the lake were an intense blue color, and the surface was soft and gentle like the underbelly of a doe.

Abu Hamid's gaze was drawn to the white birds, who'd abandoned the shore by Tiberias, fleeing in panic from the noise of the bombs. They were flying low now, looking for food.

"It's a bad situation there," Sheikh Abu Abd Allah said. "There are more Jews than Arabs."

"There are the trained Hagannah forces too," Abu Hamid said.

Suddenly the seaplane appeared in the sky, announced by the roar of its engines, the same plane with the double pairs of wings. It made a wide circle, its smoke drawing an arc in the sky, then descended and came down on its gliders, cutting a path through the water and sending up foam and spray all around. It came to a halt on the special platform between the floating barrels.

It was the first flight there for a long time, since the British evacuated the border guard camp. What was it doing there now?

"There must be some reason why it's come," said Abu Abd Allah.

Abu Hamid started feeling more bitter than ever, as though every hope was vanishing. He looked back to the lake, to the spot that had been churned up by the gliders. At that moment a boat came speeding down from the north, cutting through the waters as swiftly as the plane had.

✖

Mansour kept on watching through his binoculars: looking at Tiberias, at the buildings close to the shore and the buildings further off, at the Tournos hospital, and the secondary school, and the Lido Club. Smoke was rising somewhere in the old town, from behind the ancient walls with their covering of lichen.

Up there on the red-slated roof of the train station, abandoned now by the train and vendors and porters, he still couldn't follow a thing. All he knew was that Tiberias was like a box of matches with the matches set alight. He heard the drone of a plane, the British plane that had patrolled and transported officers when there was still a border guard camp.

Looking up into the sky, he was momentarily blinded by the bright sun. Then he spotted the arc and saw the plane descend and come down onto the water like a wild goose. Training his binoculars on the platform, he could make out the pilot's face, then he saw the boat cutting swiftly through the waves toward the plane, before finally slowing down and coming to a stop alongside. He saw the pilot talk with the man in the boat, who swung the boat around once, came back alongside and switched his engines off.

Mansour grimaced, unable to account for what was happening. The children, who loved to play in the square opposite the station, gathered around, drawn by the sound of the plane, and started talking about swimming out to it.

In the past they would have raced down to the shore in droves, to try and get one of the presents the pilot threw out. They would have flung off their clothes and plunged into the lake, then swum out to the plane to win a bar of chocolate or a packet of cookies, and the pilot would usually fling out coins, too, for them to dive for. This time, though, they hesitated, looking to one another for support. The noise of the exploding shells made them more fearful still.

They were pretty experienced, with a sense for danger, and that's why they were all conferring. Some were urging the rest on, others were saying they should be careful; some were carried away by the spirit of adventure, while others poured cold water on their enthusiasm. Torn between the two courses, they stayed there on the shore.

✖

Wolf, seeing the outer gate was open, went out through it. He'd found a bone on Khaled al-Zaher's supper plate, but it was too big for him to deal with, so he was looking for something to eat.

He went off through the narrow alleys. When he passed among some boys playing, he slowed down to watch their ball spin through the air and drop.

On he went. At the end of the alley a woman with naked breasts opened a door, carrying a pail of washing water. Afraid some man might see her hair and white bosom, she quickly threw the water out at the very moment Wolf was passing, drenching him from head to tail. He barked, and the woman hastily closed the door.

Shaking off the water, Wolf ran on in search of some sun, finally reaching the square with all its shops. It was usually crowded with people, but deserted today. He stopped in front of the butcher's shop, which was shuttered up, with no meat hanging from the hooks or grilling over the charcoal, then sat down in front of Abd al-Karim's shop, staring about him, not in the least worried by the noise of the distant shells.

He was roused by the sound of children playing, and, pricking up his ears, realized they were behind the station. He was almost dry again now, so off he went, until he was there in front of the children, who were arm in arm in a circle, pretending to be a train.

Mansour had come down from the roof now, and was sitting in the rocking chair he'd brought out from the stationmaster's office, keeping an eye on the children. Every so often he'd pull on the cigarette that never left his fingers.

Wolf sat down opposite them; they knew him, so neither he nor they were afraid. One of the children came and patted his back. After a while Wolf started leaping about with them, sometimes leading the train and sometimes tagging along behind. When the "train" went down to the shore, he started jumping about and running in front of it.

By the shore the children broke up their circle and started talking loudly, gesturing toward the plane with their hands. Then they started talking louder still, but no one took off his clothes to go into the water. Finally, seeing nothing was happening,

Wolf wandered off, passing once more in front of the station, where Mansour was sitting on the ground now, eating some food he'd brought out.

Mansour looked at the dog, then smiled and threw him a piece of bread dipped in gravy. Wolf quickly caught it, gulped it down with relish, then stood there waiting for Mansour to throw him another piece, and so it went on. When he was full, Wolf settled down, stretched his head out on the tiles and closed his eyes. The sound of the shelling had stopped.

Mansour went back to his rocking chair and gazed gently at the beautiful white dog. He remembered him as a young puppy, when Khaled al-Zaher had brought him from the head of quarantine's house. The mother had been a poodle, the father one of the local dogs, and after Khaled al-Zaher had taken him on, he'd grown by the day until he was almost as big as a small mule. And now here he was, fully grown, stretched out by the chair after his meal.

A flock of white birds settled on the red tiles of the station roof, migrating birds that came each year at this time, fleeing the cold and seeking out the warmth. What had drawn them here?

Mansour watched them from his rocking chair, while Wolf, catching the sound of their flapping wings, jumped up. It was still early morning, and the long-beaked birds were enjoying the warm sun, pluming their snowy white feathers. Mansour, not wanting to disturb them, signaled to Wolf and the dog lay down again.

The yellow car appeared in the distance, announced by the sound of its engine and soft horn, and followed by a small cloud of dust. Even this noise didn't disturb the birds, who stayed where they were. Abu Hamid got out and greeted Mansour.

"Have you seen that plane over there?" he asked.

Mansour nodded. Abu Hamid added:

"It's carrying weapons for the Jews in Tiberias. Did you see the boats?"

"I saw one."

"There are three of them now. They're moving the boxes from the plane to the boat. The old fisherman saw it with his own eyes."

The rocking of the chair stopped.

"But there aren't any explosions or shots now," Abu Hamid went on. "Something's cooking."

Mansour took a cigarette, lit it, drew on it, then blew out the smoke through his nose and mouth.

"Things are getting scary," he said. "What's the Liberation Army going to do? And the Arab states?" Then he added: "Where's the Mufti, Abu Hamid?"

"He's in Damascus, God be with him," Abu Hamid said, "trying to get arms."

Sensing, from his manner, that Mansour wasn't convinced, he started thinking of al-Taher. He could see him now, in his mind's eye, winding a white *kaffiyyeh* around his head, grenades hanging from his belt as he stood behind a barricade on one of the walls of Jerusalem.

One of the white birds took off and the rest immediately followed. Their flapping wings woke Wolf again, and he cocked his head up toward the sky, following their flight into the orchards.

"I'm going to see Abd al-Karim," Abu Hamid said. "Do you want to come with me?"

"I'm coming. Just a minute."

He quickly put the rocking chair back in the stationmaster's office and slipped on his uniform jacket. Then he shooed off the dog and hurried to the yellow car, which took off in a small cloud of dust.

✖

Wolf stood at the entrance, gazing at the place that was empty now, where the rail tracks ran off until they vanished at a spot on the horizon. He stayed there for a moment, indecisive, then circled the station, sniffing the ground, smelling the plants that sprouted all around it.

Suddenly, he heard the children again. They were coming back to their old games. Their arms outstretched, they whirled about making droning noises like the planes. Wolf sprang up, then leaped rapturously into the air. The children were imitating planes, but really they looked more like small colorful butterflies. Wolf jumped around among them and wasn't chased off.

Then, by a marvelous coincidence, the flock of white birds came back too, hovering over the station, so that there was a harmony between the movements of the arms and the flapping of the wings. The flock veered in a wide sweeping circle, then headed for the heart of the lake, as though they were greeting the children as they passed by. The children were jubilant, leaping into the air, as though intent on seizing joy in their soft hands. Wolf chased joyfully after their small light ball, jumping over a wooden barrier and showing off his skills. Then, wagging his tail, he waited his chance to join in the game once more.

It was time, though, for the children to go and get something to eat, and, one by one, they started leaving the square. Wolf was alone again, and must have remembered his home too, because off he ran, between all the closed shops, until he reached the alleyway leading to the house.

There were children playing there, and some chicks following a mother hen, who was keeping a watchful eye on a marauding cat. The woman who'd appeared bare-breasted that morning, along with the fresh smell of soap and hot water, had finished her chores now. She'd put on clean clothes and covered her head with a cotton kerchief, and was going out to make a visit.

Seeing Wolf avoid her, she must have remembered the incident earlier, because a smile flitted across her lips. She threw him a sidelong glance, then went on her way. Wolf, assailed by the sharp scent from her clothes and hair, stood and watched her pass by in her high-heeled sandals.

Feeling lonely all of a sudden, he went on himself. The stable door was open, the carriage was back, and the horse was drinking from the trough, with a bird, too, standing on the edge to take a drink. When Khaled al-Zaher came out of the stables and saw Wolf, he yelled at him, and Wolf, knowing he shouldn't have left the house for so long, slunk off into a corner of the yard.

Khaled al-Zaher, though, was a good-hearted man, and decided the reprimand was enough. He just went on with his business, ignoring the dog to show his displeasure.

In the reception room the men were sitting around talking. Hamid Abu Hamid, for the hundredth time, was telling them about the fisherman who'd witnessed, with his own eyes, the boxes of arms being passed from the plane to the boats, and swearing he himself had seen a box fall out by mistake and sink right down into the lake. Abd al-Karim arranged the broad splint across his chest, beneath his cloak, then reclined back against a cushion stuffed, in view of his condition, with wool rather than hay.

Laid out in front of them was a machine gun, a tommy gun, brought by the elementary school teacher, Ustadh* Amin, as a pledge of commitment from the National Committee. The Committee had sounded a general alert, and the crier had made the rounds of the small town, calling on anyone with arms to attend a meeting that evening.

Haj Mahmoud Shteiwi, the leader of the fighters in the 1936 revolt, was personally overseeing the digging of trenches and the building of fortifications parallel to the train tracks. There wasn't,

* *Ustadh*: Title of respect commonly given to teachers and professors.

though, any military organization in the place.

"In the future," Haj Hussein said, "we'll need to build up an organized force."

"Al-Taher will be back some day," Hamid Abu Hamid said. "He'll soon get things running."

"If you joined the local defense group," said Ustadh Amin, "that would help solve things."

Mansour sighed and said:

"The train will be back one day. It'll be back."

The sound of the plane's engines reached them on the winds, and Radi, rushing off to the roof, saw the plane skimming the surface of the lake. The boats had vanished without a trace.

The plane took off and made a wide arc heading north. The horse shied and stopped drinking, and the bird flew off. Wolf went into the stable, then over to the wall, and cocked his leg.

Chapter Ten

From the account of Abd al-Rahman the Iraqi

Asad al-Shahba was back after a week away—back from the land of jasmine and basil and damask roses, bringing a box of dried fruit and a box of *barazik** covered with sesame. He looked uneasy, apparently anxious and loath to speak.

"What's up, Asad al-Shahba?" we asked.

After some hesitation, he started telling us about Captain Ma'moun's funeral. There'd been a brass band, wreaths, a funeral cortege, scout regiments, an emissary from the Defense Ministry, a representative from the commander-in-chief, relatives of the deceased, women in funeral clothes . . .

We spent the evening listening to all this, about the burial rites and the reception for mourners who'd come from all parts of Damascus and from all over Syria. He described everything, including the various personages who either attended the funeral or came later to offer their condolences.

Finally his eyes, and ours too, were full of tears, as we felt a

* *Barazik*: Cookies made with flour or semolina and butter.

new sense of loss at the departure of a hero we'd known personally, who'd been so full of courage, holding his rifle aloft to storm a land aflame.

✖

Next day he got the presents out of his bag. He opened the box of dried fruit, and gave us all some of those delicious fruits that taste like nothing so much as the dried apricot paste in a Baghdadi breakfast. Then he gave us each some cotton underwear.

While I was chewing on the fruit, he asked:

"Have you heard from Najib?"

We fell silent. There were five men sitting in the tent with us, and they all loved Najib and kept asking anxiously about him.

"He's there," one said. "Helping defend the old city."

"He's fighting behind the walls," said another.

"He'll come back some day," a third said. "He must come back."

But the fact was, no one had seen him, and no one knew what had happened to him. Was he still alive, or had his soul ascended to heaven? No one knew. Our eyes met, each of us silently praying God would protect him, that his heart would be full of strength and his mind at rest, wherever he was.

We spent that evening recalling the battles we'd fought in, the tight corners we'd been in, the shortage of weapons, and the anxieties of the platoons and groups – the circumstances blocking the arming of more volunteers.

On the third night Asad al-Shahba took from his pocket an amulet folded in a triangle and wrapped in a green cloth, the amulet Malak had given him to ward off evil. Obviously he'd had sudden thoughts of her. What had brought her to his mind on that third night?

He wanted, it seemed, to tell me about his renewed relationship with her, but couldn't bring himself to reveal such intimate things.

He put the amulet back in the pocket of his shirt, on the left side of his chest, just above the heart.

✖

That same night, just after midnight, we got the order to return at once to the outskirts of Jerusalem. We'd heard news of the battles from official reports issued by the high command and broadcast by the army radio. There were battles on the Tulkarm front and in the Afula region, and hostilities at Zarain. Jaffa, Haifa, Beisan, Tiberias, and Safad were all in imminent danger.

The convoy moved off at daybreak. We'd got used, now, to the constant moving and stopping, the lack of sleep and the obstacles, and the shortage of weapons and ammunition.

Along with us was a company of volunteers from Yemen, Tunisia, Libya, Algeria and Morocco, who'd been hurriedly trained and were, so we were told, to be attached to the high command to give it more experience.

Asad al-Shahba and I were sitting opposite one another on a troop carrier pulling a field cannon, the only soldiers in it. In the fresh morning breeze, laden with the scent of the fields and wild flowers and dew-laden grass, he started to talk, and I listened intently.

The field cannon tied to the carrier had reminded him of the one they'd tied to the carriage, on which Captain Ma'moun's body had lain, and he went back to describing the funeral, and the delegations that had come to pay their respects. He'd gone himself, with his uncle, to a house of mourning overflowing with people.

"When my uncle heard I was escorting Captain Ma'moun's body," he said, "he came to the Kiswa area to receive us, along with a lot of other people. There was a big crowd waiting for us. There were horsemen and hired cars and motorcycles, and there were old fighters from al-Guta, and followers of Sheikh

Muhammad al-Ashmar and Sheikh Sultan Basha al-Atrash.

"The fighters kept firing rounds in the air in honor of the martyr, and the funeral turned into a big demonstration. In the middle of the tumult I felt a hand on my shoulder. It was my uncle, who embraced me with the tears rolling down his cheeks.

"Late that night we went back to my uncle's house in the old city, and I fell fast asleep. I had to wake early, though, to have a bath, and I found my uncle's wife had washed my clothes and made breakfast for us. For the first time in months I ate eggplant pressed in oil, and yogurt spread, and quince jam.

"My uncle didn't go to work that morning. He'd arranged to go to the funeral with old Hadou, who came after breakfast and drank coffee with us. Then, putting our trust in God, we left to take part in the funeral.

"I didn't allow myself to think too much of Malak, or even ask about her. I was too caught up in the funeral—the only topic of conversation was the circumstances of Captain Ma'moun's martyrdom. Even my uncle's wife, who usually did all she could to get me onto the subject, respected my solemn mood of mourning. She didn't mention Malak or even make any hints about her.

"The funeral rites took place in the Martyrs' Cemetery, and I lost sight of my uncle in the crowds. I hitched a ride on the truck carrying the military band, got off at Bab al-Musalli and walked on to his house. In fact, I got there before him, and my uncle's wife made me a glass of lemonade, then hurried back to the kitchen to put the finishing touches on the meal she was slowly cooking.

"We all met together around the lunch table, my uncle and Uncle Hadou and myself. We ate without any appetite, each of us plunged deep in his thoughts. Afterwards my uncle made another effort to get some conversation moving, asking me about the war in Palestine and the battles I'd fought in, and what would happen when the Arab armies intervened after the British had left.

"Somehow God inspired me to talk. I spoke about the war and

the different kinds of fighting, about all the different sorts of weapons, and military planning and execution. I described the plains and the mountains, the flowers and plants, the villages and settlements, the moments of fear and anxiety, the times of daring and courage under fire. I talked about planes that spat out fire, and cannons that threw out lava, and mines that shook mountains.

"As I sensed my words seizing their attention, I went into more details about various things. And when I'd finished, my uncle sat there gazing at me proudly, then turned to his guest as if to say: 'You see?'

✖

"On my third day at my uncle's house, I had a surprise: I got home to find my parents had just arrived from Aleppo, after a long journey. Astonishment and a flood of emotions swept through me. We spent the evening half laughing, half in tears, and later on we were joined by Uncle Hadou and his wife. Then, after a time, Malak arrived. She had a red scarf wound around her hair, setting off her fair complexion wonderfully, and her tall, graceful body was wrapped in a Damascene gown with gold thread.

"Her visit must have been secretly arranged between her mother and my uncle's wife. All eyes were on her—it was as though an angel had come down from the heavens. Praised be God who created such beauty.

"Soon after she'd come, the men separated from the women to go up to the attic room and hear the news on the radio, and so I had no chance to look in her eyes to see if there was any reproach or indifference there. My uncle switched on the radio, which was covered with a piece of white embroidery that had, hanging from one side, a piece of alum like a crystal, and a blue bead. He fiddled with the switch until he found the Near East station that broadcast the news at that hour, and the newscaster read it out, but I didn't hear it.

I was elsewhere – trying to think up some excuse to go down and find a way of whispering in Malak's ear.

"After the news the men started talking about politics. My father, I felt, had started taking a new interest in what was going on in the world, and I was pleased events around us had drawn his attention. Relief came, finally, when my uncle's wife called to me to take the coffee tray. I hurried down, to find Malak waiting for me with the tray she'd got ready.

"Some of the light from the kitchen had filtered out into the courtyard, and she was standing there near the fountain. She looked at me boldly, and I stood face to face with her, without the usual barrier of the black georgette veil.

"'It's been a long time,' she said reproachfully, in the sternest tones she could muster.

"I realized then how wrong I'd been, in pretending to have forgotten her. I didn't answer, trying, instead, to memorize her features – to take in the blackness of her eyes and the delicacy of the brows, the tenderness of her lips and the bloom on her cheeks. With so little time, this 'chance' meeting had to be put to good use. I found myself hastily whispering: 'I'll wait for you tomorrow, at Marjeh Square, before noon.'

"As I took the tray from her, my fingers brushed against hers and I felt everything inside me trembling, so much that I spilled some coffee onto the gold-rimmed saucers."

The convoy was passing along some rough dirt roads, and that broke up the conversation. We had to hold onto our seats and keep our feet firmly pressed down to stop ourselves from falling off.

We reached the headquarters at Zarain, and the new volunteers got down. Then another company joined us, under the command of Colonel Nour al-Din, who was wearing a military jacket adorned with medals and stars. We had a light meal while waiting for the trucks to be loaded and refueled.

The glow on Asad al-Shahba's face, while he was talking about his personal affairs, had gone now. He was looking serious. Colonel Nour al-Din, with his swarthy face, passed by swaggering like a peacock. I recalled the bullet-proof vest Najib had talked about, which had passed from hand to hand until it finally reached Colonel Nour al-Din. I'd told Asad al-Shahba about the vest, and he laughed as he remembered how Ahmad Bey had claimed it was booty from the battle of al-Ziraa.

When the convoy started up again, our carrier had filled with soldiers and boxes of ammunition.

Our target was the Jerusalem area, where the Jews were attacking relentlessly to try and gain control of the city and the roads leading to it. We were to join in the fight and block their assaults until the regular Arab armies arrived. We reached our position at last, around sunset.

A forward party came to meet us, and we halted. We had some armored cars and seven-and-a-half-inch mortar guns. We were met by the locals with cheers and songs, and food and drink.

Our allotted position was at al-Khan al-Ahmar, and Colonel Nour al-Din told us we made up the mobile reserve troops, ready to go to any position where help was needed, under the personal leadership of the commander-in-chief.

We set up camp at the foot of the hill alongside the Jerusalem-Jericho road, with Jerusalem just beyond it. We were beyond the range of their artillery, but we were kept on full alert, fingers on triggers when we weren't asleep. The region was bedouin, and we had fresh milk to drink and learned camel riding.

One evening, after guard duty was over, we started walking up and down the main camp area. First I'd talk while Asad al-Shahba listened, and then the roles would be mostly reversed.

Suddenly he picked up the conversation that had been interrupted before.

"I waited for her at Marjeh Square," he went on, "but she didn't come. I waited for a long time, casting my shadow on the pavement looking over the river Barada, then circling around the fountain in the middle, but it was no use. She hadn't come. Why?

"Still I waited, finally dragging myself home in the evening. Where was she? I passed in front of her windows, but they were closed; there was no trace of her. I knocked on my uncle's door—and it was Malak who opened.

"She'd wound her veil around her hair, and she gave me a sly look, as though she knew what I must be feeling after such a long wait. I went in, to find the place full of women: my mother, my uncle's wife, Malak, and her mother and younger sister. I sat down with them, stealing glances at Malak, trying to say, with my eyes: 'So that's the way you treat me!' And every time our eyes met, she'd give me that same sly smile to taunt me.

"I gathered from what the women were saying that they'd decided to recite from the Life of the Prophet to celebrate my safe return. I seized a fleeting moment, as I stood with her at the fountain, filling the brass cup with water scented with lemon leaves, to ask her why she hadn't come. She laughed right out, then said teasingly:

"'Isn't it enough we're seeing one another here?'

✖

"In the evening the women started wrapping up sweets in white paper and tying them with colored string. Then, after evening prayers, they began their recital from the Quran, and my father, my uncle and I left for the house of our neighbor Uncle Hadou, because it wasn't proper for men to stay in a house where women were raising their voices.

"We sat in a big reception room, on luxurious Damascene chairs delicately carved with the shapes of stars and moons and inlaid with mother-of-pearl. That night I saw Malak's older brother Ziyad, who was thirty years old and mentally retarded. Usually he sat in a side room, plunged in silence, just letting out a muted cry every so often for his mother or sister or brother, then lapsing into silence once more.

"It seemed he was destined to miss that evening—because he made so much noise Uncle Hadou shut him in his room. But then my father and uncle interceded for him, begging Uncle Hadou to open the door, and he not only opened it but took his son and washed his face, then brought him to sit with us.

"'This boy's a sore trial to the family,' he said.

"Ziyad sat looking at us with a foolish smile on his face, and by and by we got used to him being there. We were deep in conversation, my father talking about his restaurant, my uncle about his business, and Uncle Hadou about his leather works, when we heard the sound of the women reciting praises to heaven in unison. Ziyad started getting noisy again, calling out in his indistinct voice for his younger brother, who'd gone with his mother and sister to hear the recital and eat sweets. Uncle Hadou got annoyed then, and, afraid the evening might be spoiled, got hold of his son, took him to his room and locked him in.

"'Why don't you put him in a hospital?' my father asked. 'He'd be more comfortable there, and he'd get the care you can't give him at home.'

"My uncle agreed, backing my father up, but Uncle Hadou said nothing as a tear escaped his eye.

"Ziyad became the evening's main topic then, as Uncle Hadou started talking of the hardships for the family, of the daily pain caused by Ziyad's condition. He told us at length of the efforts to cure him, the various medicines bought, the number of tombs visited, and so on. The evening became somber and Uncle Hadou depressed.

I tried my best to liven things up, but it was no good.

✖

"When I went to bed that night, the image of that unfortunate man stayed in my mind. Every time I tried to calm myself down, I'd have that picture of the door locked in his face. All I could see was his face, with his fair hair, light complexion and handsome features. Little did I know circumstances were to make this luckless boy a source of concern to others, that he was due, by fate and chance, to dominate the final days of my leave.

"Ziyad left the house without his family having any inkling. His mother was doing the laundry, and the washroom was full of steam and the smell of soap, with the noise of the kerosene stove drowning every other sound. As for Malak, she was darning the family's socks in her room, which took her all morning. And so the retarded young man, finding the door open, simply walked out.

"The alley was empty and he walked along, passing from one alley to the next, until finally he emerged into the street. No one noticed he'd gone until the younger son came back from school. He went to his brother's room, then, not finding him there, looked all over the house for him, in the storeroom, under the stairs, behind the jasmine tree, by the swing, but still he couldn't find him. He was panic-stricken. 'Ziyad's gone!' he shouted. 'Ziyad's gone!'

"Malak heard her younger brother shouting, threw down her work and rushed to see what the matter was. She too looked here, there and everywhere, then, exhausted, let out a loud cry, which her mother caught over the noise of the stove, striking fear into her heart. She wiped her arms clean and jumped to her feet, then she in turn searched, coming and going frantically until she collapsed weeping.

"When the sound of her sobbing and wailing reached the neighboring houses, all the women, starting with my uncle's wife and my mother, gathered around, and the news was swiftly taken to the shop of Uncle Hadou, who rushed off to the police and hospitals. Passing by my uncle's shop in al-Hamidiyyeh, where I was sitting too, he broke the news to us.

"My uncle slapped his hands together, and said: 'There is no power or strength except in God.' Then he got up right away and closed the shop, suggesting we should all look for the boy in different parts and meet at home in the evening. I searched in al-Shagur and on the outskirts of al-Guta, but found no trace of him.

"The men were sitting on cane chairs at the entrance to the quarter, hopeless despair written on their faces. As they saw me return alone, they didn't even ask me how my search had gone. They could see the result in my face. I sat there with the rest of them, as they discussed the matter to the point of exhaustion. The only hope was of hearing something from the police, who'd informed all their centers of the matter.

"No one slept much that night. As I got ready for bed, I thought of Malak, picturing her pale face and red eyes. That retarded boy, forgotten in his room, had suddenly become precious when he disappeared. No one had felt his presence, but what an emptiness he'd left behind him!

"All next day we waited for news of Ziyad, and the sorrow grew in our neighbors' house, the atmosphere totally despondent. On the third day after the disappearance, my parents decided to go back to Aleppo. As I kissed their hands at the door of the coach, my mother wept until she was choked by her tears, and kept uttering prayers for me and making vows for my safe return.

"After they'd gone, I decided there was no reason for me to stay either, that I should return to base. The night before I was due to leave, my uncle went to the mosque for evening prayers, while his wife went to the neighbors' house.

"And so I was alone when there was a knock on the door and Malak came in. She took one step inside, leaving the outer door half open, then stopped. She was wearing a filmy headscarf, and her face was tired. Ziyad had still not come back, and the thing was clearly beginning to get her down, though she was doing her best to be firm and patient.

"'Are you leaving us before Ziyad comes back?' she whispered.

"With a feeling of weakness I grasped her hand, that hand colored with henna, holding it between both my own. She quickly pulled it back, then half-turned, looked at me over her shoulder, and said: 'God be with you and keep you safe.' Then she opened the door and went back, leaving a vast well of emptiness behind her.

"I don't know how I got through that evening. My uncle and his wife did their best to cheer me up, trying to change the atmosphere that had weighed us down since Ziyad vanished. She quickly made some *zalabia** and put a bowl of fruit in front of us, and my uncle, for the first time since the incident, switched on the radio, filling the room with the voice of Asmahan. The change, though, was all on the surface. Deep inside us there was bitter sorrow.

"Still, the next morning I said goodbye to them and left, feeling lost as I walked along the silent alley. The city streets were empty too. There was no one out that early, except for garbage men collecting the trash.

"As the bus started for Quneitra, my point for moving on to Palestine, I tried to convince myself the mission I'd dedicated myself to was nobler than any personal matters. In any case, I thought, I'd soon be back in the atmosphere of war and forget about it."

---

* *Zalabia*: A fritter soaked in syrup

Asad al-Shahba fell silent, his story finished. I'd been listening all ears as he recounted those small details he must have been going over constantly in his mind. Had he managed to forget after all, plunged in the atmosphere of war?

How sharp one's senses grew in these wildernesses! How delightful the memory of such small details became! And how men's dreams strove to reawaken what was lost in deepest slumber!

Chapter Eleven

Tiberias fell after bitter fighting; it fell, and its people fled to Samakh, a few in cars and trucks, most on foot. People kept pouring toward Samakh, relentlessly, flooding out from behind the smoke. You could see them from the heights of Jisr Bab al-Toum, carrying what few belongings they could manage amid the crying of children and women's tears. They'd stop from time to time, to have a drink of water or check their children, but there was no break in the wailing and crying.

Abd al-Karim turned over in bed and opened the attic window, as new arrivals filled the streets and the spacious square and the station building. News of the disaster was spreading like wildfire. Mansour, still wearing his uniform with the brass buttons, sat by his bed, sipping the last of his coffee and talking.

For two weeks now the battle had been raging fiercely. It had started in the old city quarters between the inhabitants and Jewish forces of the Golani Brigade, with the cursed British reinforcing them with arms and explosives via the steamboats. The Jews had started by occupying Sheikh Qaddumi's Hill west of Tiberias, and the village of Nasser al-Din, cutting it off from Loubia and stopping relief from reaching it. After bitter fighting the Jewish forces had managed to cut the old city in two and so overpower the fighters and inhabitants who were defending the city.

That was how Mansour had summed up the battle, and he'd been repeating the same account for two days now. As for Abd al-Karim, he'd become used to disasters and wasn't expecting any good news. He saw everything in his dreams as he slept.

Radi came down from the attic and into the room, his manner agitated. "The refugees have filled the beach area by the shore," he said. Mansour nodded sadly, as if knowing it would be Samakh's turn next.

The people were thronging the shoreline, hoping, perhaps, for a last look at their homes on the other side. Mansour gazed out of the window at the sky, the rosary moving rhythmically beneath his fingers. The smell of *taboun* bread, quickly made, wafted up from below, where Umm Radi and Fatima were baking, while Khaled al-Zaher loaded the bread onto the cart to distribute among the new arrivals.

The town was plunged into turmoil as still more people from Tiberias poured in, filling the streets with clamor, carts, luggage and children. The square was full, the courtyard of the mosque was full, and so were all the paths leading to al-Hammeh.

Hamid Abu Hamid, spurred on by a sense of honor, drove his yellow car along the dirt road, to avoid the crowds thronging the main one, leaving a trail of dust behind him.

There at Bab al-Toum the old people were gathered, the ones who couldn't go on walking, waiting for carts to pick them up. Quite a few of them had been there since the night before, huddled in woolen wraps and looking back with tearful eyes, heaving one sigh after another. The wind was blowing over Tiberias from the east, carrying the stench of smoke and fire.

Abu Hamid rolled up his sleeves and opened the car doors wide, to let in ten old people who somehow crammed inside. He took them to the town, set them down at the National Committee headquarters, then set off once more. He kept going back and forth, not even thinking of his gas supply, until the gas suddenly ran out on the outskirts of Bab al-Toum. The car wouldn't move another inch.

There were still a lot of people waiting, still needing help. He kept trying to start the car, but it was no use—there wasn't a drop left in the tank. Where could he get any gas at a time like this? There was no gas in Tiberias, or Beisan. Usually, when things were tense and he ran out, he'd seek out one of his acquaintances at the border guard camp, but where could he go now? He opened the door and got out. He was a mile from Jisr al-Bab and a few more from Samakh.

He looked around him, seeing more scattered groups of people on the move. A flock of the white birds passed, hovering close to the ground. He could hear the flapping of their wings quite clearly. Those birds could smell danger, and they showed their fear by moving from one area to another, without ever folding their wings or nestling their heads on their breasts, to give themselves a rest.

Just my luck! Abu Hamid thought, and wondered what to do. Before long he'd closed the windows, locked the car doors and started his walk back, along a dirt track passing through orchards not far from the settlement of Degania. He made his way carefully, keeping a firm grip on his car keys on their chain of blue beads.

Still he walked on, then turned around to look at the yellow car. It was the first time he'd ever left his car after a breakdown. Usually he'd wait alongside it, guarding it until another car came along and offered some help. He remembered the night of the hyenas, with Abd al-Karim al-Hamad. This time, though, it was different: the country was being lost, the disasters piling up.

The path wound this way and that, and he walked with his keys clasped in his hand, his eyes whipped by an east wind that had sprung up suddenly, carrying grains of sand and the smell of burning. What should he do, he wondered? There was no hope of gas in the present situation, so the best thing would be to find another car and get a few gallons from it. Either that, or find a cart to tow his car to the town.

Suddenly he heard the sound of crying, the sharp crying of a baby coming up from the grass, piercing the heart. He looked all around and realized, finally, it was coming from behind a nearby licorice tree.

He raced across the straw and thorns, and found the baby there, wrapped in a white cloth, crying and then stopping, as if imploring help, its face blue—perhaps it had been crying for a long time. He bent down and picked it up, then cradled it against his chest, upon which it quieted down and twisted around, as if looking for its mother's breast.

He'd never had any children himself. Now he was swept, overwhelmingly, by feelings of suppressed fatherhood. Obviously hungry and thirsty, the child was opening its mouth, the way fish do, but he had nothing to give it. He looked around again, wondering how a baby had come to such a place.

The citizens of Tiberias had, he knew, taken many different paths. He'd seen people, alone or in groups, cutting across country tracks to the nearby villages. What chance had flung this baby here by the side of the path? Where was its mother, its father?

His gaze fell on a piece of white cloth hanging on a dried-up thorny bush, where the wind had swept it and then entangled it. Perhaps, he thought, the mother had put the baby there to go and look for food or water, and she'd be back soon. If she came back to find her baby gone, she'd be distraught.

The white cloth was a woman's head cover, but where was the

poor woman herself? The baby was quiet now, still opening its mouth in search of the nipple. Tenderly he cuddled it, realizing it must have been there under the licorice tree for quite a while. Its wrappings were soaked through, and the smell made it only too clear why.

He kept walking around, still trying to find some trace of the mother. He thought he saw her tracks on the soil and dry scrub, but he couldn't follow them because a flock of sheep had trampled the area, wiping out the traces. Best, he thought, to wait there for a while and hope she'd turn up. Suddenly he felt the keys in his hand, and remembered his car. Seeing someone else's misfortune, he reflected, taught you to bear your own. After a long wait, he finally decided to go home. He picked up the headdress, wrapped it around the baby and hurried off before it got dark.

✖

As he walked through the front door of his house, his wife, who'd been preparing food in the kitchen and smelled of garlic, saw what he was carrying and stopped dead. Then she approached him, hardly able to believe her eyes.

"Where did this baby come from?" she asked.

"I found it."

"Where?"

"Out in the open. In the fields."

She stretched out her arms and cradled it.

"Careful," he said. "It's asleep."

It had indeed fallen asleep during the long walk, feeling safe and closing its eyes the moment it was in someone's arms. The woman looked at it, and, as her deep motherly feelings woke, her face started blooming.

"How did you find it? Where? How did it happen?"

She asked endless questions, which he answered as patiently

as he could. Not satisfied, she took the baby off to see to it, while Abu Hamid washed his hands and face and went to the pantry to find some food, not waiting for what was simmering on the stove.

As he ate he decided what to do. He'd go to the mosque and ask the *muezzin* to announce the discovery. That might be the quickest way to find the baby's parents and family. Then he thought of his car and was filled with worry again. It was nearly evening, and it would be dark soon. How on earth was he going to get back to the place where he'd left it, close by Degania and Shaar Ha-Golan?

He squatted on the lambskin, turning matters over in his mind, unable to reach a final decision. When his wife came back, she was carrying the baby, changed now, wrapped in a clean cloth.

"It's a baby girl," she said. "She's a lovely baby," she added gaily, twirling the child about in the middle of the room. "So pretty!" Then she said:

"I've given her some sugar and water, but it's milk she needs."

He was about to say he'd go off and find some, but she said: "She needs breast milk, from a nursing mother."

She'd never even been pregnant herself, and her breast was completely dry. What could they do?

"Our neighbor's nursing a girl this age," she said. "I'll take her there before it gets dark." She hurried inside to get a head cover, then, telling him to be sure to take the pot off the fire at the right time, went off.

Abu Hamid got up, performed his ablutions and put on his shoes. Then, as he raised his eyes, his gaze fell on the picture of the Mufti that was hanging on the wall. They stared at one another, the Mufti with his calm face and serene air and Abu Hamid with all the turmoil churning inside him. He looked at the picture for a long time, as though urging or imploring. Then he took the pot off the fire and left in his turn.

He walked over to the mosque, where he performed his evening prayers and asked the *muezzin* to make an announcement from the minaret, about the lost baby girl at his house. Then he went to Haj Hussein's reception room, sounding the brass knocker on the outer gate and entering with the words: "God protect us."

The place was buzzing with people, with, in the forefront, six men from Sama al-Rousan, Malka and Irbid who had come wearing belts of cartridges and carrying rifles to defend their homeland.

He gave his greetings, then sat down and waited for the right moment to ask Haj Hussein to send Khaled al-Zaher with him, before dawn, to tow back the broken-down car from the outskirts of Bab al-Toum.

All the talk was of the events in Tiberias and what was going to happen now in Samakh—because Samakh would be next! Abu Hamid had plenty of chances to mention his car, but preferred to talk to Haj Hussein about it when people had gone. Only they didn't go. They just went on talking, one story getting entangled with the next, one incident bringing another to mind. Then, finally, Mansour came in his navy blue uniform and abruptly told everyone that the Jews were advancing toward the outskirts of the town under cover of darkness.

There was silence as the men stopped talking. Everyone was dejected, the faces wan and anxious. Mansour told them what he'd heard from the people of the Manshiyyeh quarter, then Salim al-Aid came from the National Committee and confirmed the news.

"What are we waiting for?" Haj Hussein said.

As one man they leaped up and shouldered their rifles.

When Abu Hamid got home, he found his wife was back too, occupied with the baby who'd had a full drink of milk at the breast of their neighbor Nazima. She'd forgotten about herself and everything around her, giving all her energy to this child who'd appeared from nowhere.

She was lulling the baby to sleep, and motioned to him not to make a noise. He went straight to the cupboard and took out his rapid-firing rifle; then, from the wooden chest where his wife kept all her precious linen and embroideries, he took out his leather ammunition belt. He gazed at the picture of the Mufti hanging on the wall, to inspire himself with resolve and good heart.

His wife looked at him, with eyes that held a lot of questions and a touch of fear too. He made a reassuring gesture, then put on the leather belt with its pouches full of ammunition, seized his automatic rifle and went out. His wife, having first made sure the baby was asleep, followed him into the courtyard. At the outer gate, she asked:

"Where are you going?"

Getting no reply, she followed him out.

"Where's the car?" she asked anxiously.

"I'll explain everything later," he said, without turning around. Then he strode off to the headquarters of the National Committee.

The men were digging trenches behind the rail tracks that divided the town in two, digging, filling sacks with soil and building barricades. The battle was at hand now, and their lives hung in the balance.

The townspeople were spread out all along the train tracks, the houses behind them silent and unlit, while the monotonous sounds of the field insects, the grasshoppers and the crickets, and the frogs with their insistent croaking, only served to make the night more desolate.

Silence had closed in on Tiberias too. Its lights, which had glowed from afar like a string of pearls, were extinguished now.

The silence was oppressive and the night heavy, with no one to light a lantern or lift his voice in song. An anxious silence settled over the sky, over the whole earth. Only the waves still rustled as though with the wings of birds.

Mansour spun around, his gun on his shoulder, passing the different lookout posts, which were quite close together, greeting people and walking on until he reached the station. He wasn't alone there. There was a Bren gun fixed on the rooftop, and a team of three men filling sacks to reinforce the position.

Abu Hamid stopped by, and Mansour asked him eagerly:

"What's happening?"

Abu Hamid was aware how people said he had secret links with the Mufti's party and knew everything that was going on. He laughed, and said:

"Look out! The Jews are coming!"

Mansour spun around the rocking chair he'd brought from the stationmaster's office. "Sit down," he said.

Abu Hamid sat, happy to have a rest after his long day.

"I hear your car broke down near Bab al-Toum," Mansour said.

Abu Hamid said nothing, though a pang went through him.

"I heard too," Mansour went on, "that you found a baby out in the fields."

Again he didn't answer, recalling the soft face, tender fingers and honey eyes. Mansour, realizing Abu Hamid didn't feel like talking, fell silent too.

✖

The time passed slowly. Finally it was midnight, the grasshoppers, crickets and frogs still keeping up their chirping and croaking. As for the men behind the barricades, they were quiet now, striving to stay on full alert.

As the time dragged on, Abu Hamid started feeling sleepy,

while Mansour spread his woolen cover on the floor and stretched out to take a short rest. There was no movement or sound from the three men sitting behind the Bren gun.

Suddenly a bomb fell somewhere behind them. Abu Hamid woke, his finger on the trigger, and sprang to his feet, while Mansour too leaped up. The two men shivered, hearing voices coming from different directions.

Another bomb fell, nearer this time. Then, suddenly, there was shooting from all directions, and heavy firing lit up the horizon. People started talking.

"They're fighting at al-Manshiyyeh."

"Don't waste your ammunition."

"Move forward, to the front line."

Abu Hamid felt the strength flooding through him. He leaped over the low wall and rushed to the front positions, brandishing his gun, hurling himself forward to meet this ogre who was showing his claws.

✖

Voices sounded and resounded. Voices of people and a hail of bullets.

The men cried out to encourage one another, and there was a whining of bullets, flying back and forth, echoing down into the depths of the lake. No one knew quite what was happening; anxiety hung over everyone. There was a movement of branches on the trees, and the surging of the waves, and the quivering movement of fish in the deep.

In his attic room Abd al-Karim al-Hamad was sitting up in bed, listening to the sounds that reached him from a distance. He still had the brace around his chest, in which he seemed to feel the strangled roars of caged lions. The people of the house went down and hid in the stables: Khadijeh with her baby, Fatima, Radi and large numbers of women and children from the neighboring houses.

When the shooting started, Haj Hussein had come and said: "Don't worry, Abd al-Karim." Then he'd grasped his hand, as if to say: don't worry, Abd al-Karim, we'll beat them. His rifle was hanging from his shoulder, and he'd flung back the sides of his headdress and lifted his gown, tucking its edges under his belt. He had the aura of a man who has performed the pilgrimage.

And so he left, along with the other men, while Abd al-Karim, stayed on here, alone with the women and children. A tear escaped his eye, and all the time the needles of pain pierced his chest and ribs.

Khadijeh came in carrying her baby Maher, intent on having a word with him too, but she held back when she saw his face, drawn with anxiety. Don't worry about stray bullets or bombs dropping from the sky, that look of his said. Don't worry about all that. There's a far deadlier bomb exploding inside me.

Next Fatima came, trembling in her terror. "Go back to the stables," he told her. She didn't answer, but she didn't leave either.

The terror of that dark night, when Qassem al-Nayyef was killed, was visible on her face; it was clear she was prey to dreadful thoughts. She sat down on the floor in a corner, not daring, any more than Khadijeh, to go down to the stables for protection. She just sat there without a word, and he knew well enough she was thinking of their old home.

He felt a longing, too, for the House of Peace, which he hadn't entered since it had come within range of enemy fire. Were the water conduits for the tomatoes and eggplant caked up now? Had the basil and the *qarn al-ghazal** and the lavender flowers wilted? Had the damask rose bushes and the vines dried up? And how about—

Must the secret stay locked in his injured chest?

"Fatima, listen," he called, trying to adjust his position. Fatima

* *qarn al-ghazal*: Local flower, somewhat similar to a tulip.

leaped up and hurried over to help, plumping up the pillow behind him and helping him lean back. He thought of saying nothing after all, but she was leaning over him, ready to listen attentively.

"Listen," he said. "I'm going to tell you a secret."

She kept her eyes fixed on him, waiting for him to go on.

"I hid my savings," he went on. "Some pieces of gold and some money. An ounce of gold, a hundred guineas, three rings and a solid gold bracelet."

"Where did you hide them?" she broke in, urging him on with a movement of her hand.

He felt ashamed. Here are people fighting, he thought, and all I can think of is my money. Sensing his feelings, Fatima grew less insistent, leaving him to say what he wanted at his own pace. After a pause, he said:

"I hid it in the garden of the house, five steps from the threshold and three steps from the lemon tree. I wrapped it in a nylon bag, dug a hole a meter deep and buried it there."

He looked up into her face to see her reaction, and, as he expected, saw her face had darkened. Here was another burden for her to carry.

"Did anyone see you ?" she asked.

He recalled how Qassem al-Nayyef had seen him digging and hiding the bag on that dark night, but he didn't want to add to her sorrows by reminding her of her dead husband.

"No," he said. "No one else knows."

"When the fighting's over," she said, with a determined ring in her voice, "I'll go over there and fetch it all."

Suddenly Radi came in.

"Stay in the stables," she shouted, thrusting him back. "Can't you hear the bullets?" She'd forgotten her fear now, even though the fighting was getting closer.

"Let him be, Fatima," Abd al-Karim said. "He isn't a child any more."

Radi sat down on the edge of the bed, and Fatima, who'd been anxious to ply Abd al-Karim with questions about the buried treasure, decided not to say anything more in front of the boy. The sound of shooting, coming closer now, woke Wolf, who started barking intermittently.

✖

It was getting nearer, and the alleys were full of din and confusion. When the news came, it spread panic.

The defenders of the Manshiyyeh quarter had been forced to retreat before the fierce Jewish attack; Salim al-Saadi had fallen a martyr, ten men had been wounded and the inhabitants had to leave the quarter. As for the flocks and herds that had grazed there, the animals were all dead, and the rail tracks were the town's last defense now. Everyone's morale was shaken.

The Bren gun was moved from the station rooftop to the roof of the National Committee building. The Jews unleashed a heavy bombardment, blowing up the houses in the areas they captured. The sound of the explosions shook the town. One bomb fell near the station, fragments from it cannoning into the tiles of the roof, which crashed down and smashed.

As the defenders retreated to their fortifications, behind the rail tracks, the Jews advanced, their voices clearly audible as they chattered away in Hebrew. It was a bitter moment. A member of the National Committee addressed the men alongside him.

"If we don't stop them," he said, "they'll kill us and rip open our women's bellies."

From the depths of the night, borne on a sudden gust of wind, came the sound of a woman's ululation, splitting the night in two. She'd come from the furthest part of the town, and when she reached the fortified positions she let out her ululation and cried:

"God is great!"

More ululations poured out from behind windows and from beyond the darkness. Enthusiasm reached fever pitch. The men unleashed their bullets and the young men leaped over the barricades to meet their enemies, who were boldly advancing.

✖

"Aunt Hafiza's fighting with the men," Radi said. "They say," he added, "she came on foot from the Duwair estate when she heard about the attack."

Abd al-Karim, who'd left his bed, considered leaving the attic to find out what was going on. The cries and weeping from the stables were getting on his nerves. He'd called to Fatima, but she hadn't heard him.

"Aunt Hafiza's still with them," Radi went on. Abd al-Karim wished now he'd kept the rifle he'd taken from the soldier. The fighting seemed to be going on right underneath the window.

Still Radi kept talking to him, showing no sign of fear, and in spite of everything he found himself smiling at the boy. God knows, Radi, he thought, what lies in wait for you!

Toward the end of the night the voices died away. The shelling and the bombing stopped, and there was just some intermittent shooting. The Jews had failed to penetrate the last line of defense, and they were retreating with the first streaks of light. No one in the town had slept. By the time dawn came, all the shooting had stopped.

Chapter Twelve

Worn out at last, Abd al-Karim closed his eyes and slept. His sleep, though, was troubled, more like a faint. When he opened his eyes, he found Radi in front of him.

"They didn't get into the town," Radi said. He'd evidently been waiting there for a long time. In a voice burning with enthusiasm, he added:

"Father came back an hour ago, after the fighting stopped. His gown and his pants were all covered in mud. He'd been fighting all night."

Abd al-Karim opened his eyes, beginning to understand. He raised himself onto his elbows, his heart pounding.

"Is it really true?" he said.

"Father came back with the barrel of his rifle hot, from all the endless shooting."

He paused for a minute then added:

"My aunt Hafiza's come back too. She's got her head wrapped in a *kaffiyyeh* and an army belt around her waist."

"Help me get up," Abd al-Karim said, bracing himself for the effort.

He kept his nightdress on, but put on his Damascene cloak over it.

"Are they in the reception room now?" he asked.

The boy nodded his head. Abd al-Karim opened the window, letting in air heavy with the spray from the lake's waves, then sat down on a chair in the corner, while Radi sat himself on the edge of the bed.

"I didn't sleep at all last night," Radi said. "I just waited. Then, when the fighting stopped, I went out in the courtyard. The rabbits were already there, jumping around, as if the smell of gunpowder had upset them."

Khaled al-Zaher had already flung the big outer gate wide open, so, he said, that the men could walk in with their heads high after the night's fighting. They'd announced their return with a lot of noise, his father at their head, and now they came in, heads erect, with their rifles and ammunition, their clothes all soiled by the mud and earth.

They went straight through to the reception room, which they entered with pride and dignity, talking of all the things that had happened. They piled their shoes up by the threshold, then slept there, in their clothes, with their rifles by their sides. Aunt Hafiza came in after the men, talking boldly with them, and they praised her, calling her a heroine and the sister of men.

The father couldn't sleep. He performed the dawn prayers, then sat in meditation, fingering the beads of his rosary, while Aunt Hafiza woke the women of the house and urged them to prepare breakfast for the men.

If only I had a rifle, Abd al-Karim thought to himself. Oh, how I wish I'd kept that rifle.

He thought of the dagger hidden in Umm Radi's cupboard. He'd better keep that by him, he reflected. After all, who knew how things were going to turn out?

"I heard them say the Jews are going to attack again," Radi said,

as more spray-laden air blew in. "And I heard them asking – where are the Arab armies? Where's al-Kawuqji, and where's Haj Amin?"

A rooster crowed, then came the voice of Aunt Hafiza calling out, and Radi realized breakfast was ready. Soon they heard the sound of footsteps on the stairs, and Fatima came in carrying some pancakes in honey.

"Good morning, Uncle."

"Good morning, Fatima."

She put the plate down on the small table, noticing how he was sitting on a chair wrapped in the Damascene cloak he'd always worn at sunset under the trellis in the orchard, in those good, quiet days in the House of Peace. She was anxious about the money hidden there, and kept turning the matter over and over in her mind.

"You'd better eat the pancakes," she said, "while they're still hot."

Suddenly there was the explosion of a shell, sounding like thunder. There was a whistling of wind, then the explosion shook the house and rattled the windows. Abd al-Karim still hadn't washed his face, but he didn't need to throw water on it to be wide awake now.

There was a commotion, then a sudden movement at the foot of the stairs. Had the men woken up? Had this explosion from nowhere chased the sleep from them, made them leap up to find just where it had come from?

Radi went downstairs, urged on by an instinctive fear or curiosity to know what was happening. As for Fatima, she stayed calm. She was used, now, to danger threatening from all sides. Abd al-Karim, looking out of the window, saw a column of water rising from the midst of the lake, like a cascading fountain.

"It was a big bomb," he said. "It fell in the lake."

Fatima didn't give the matter much thought. Her mind was on

the old house, and the money hidden there.

"What's the matter, Fatima?" Abd al-Karim asked, seeing how quiet she was. She answered right away.

"Listen, Uncle. This is the right time. Will you let me go and fetch the money?"

"No," he said sharply. Then he added, in a gentle voice:

"The Jews are there. You mustn't think of going."

She felt a desire for adventure, to court danger, and she wished he'd let her go. Then a feeling of peace and reassurance took hold of her. What tenderness and warmth there'd been in his voice! Emotion flooded her heart.

Another shell dropped. Where was it? Abd al-Karim, unable to guess, went on watching the lake, where the column of water had subsided now. A powerful wave surged, then crashed fiercely, churning up the surface of the lake as wave after wave followed.

A flock of the white birds that usually visited Samakh at that time of the year flew overhead, flapping their wings and making frightened screeching noises. Abd al-Karim turned.

"Go down now, Fatima," he said. "And don't even think of going to the house, you hear me?"

Fatima went down as instructed, and Abd al-Karim stayed there alone, smelling the scent of danger, feeling it in every pore. Radi came back, out of breath.

"Father says to come down to the reception room," he said.

Abd al-Karim didn't hesitate. He was eager for some indication of what was going on, and, leaning on Radi, he went down the stairs and into the reception room, to find Haj Hussein speaking anxiously to the other men. He greeted everyone, then sat down in an empty spot. It was evident there'd been worrying news.

A man from the National Committee was speaking.

"They've got field cannons now," he said, "and they're firing to test them."

Mansour came in, greeted the men and sat down. He asked

Abd al-Karim how he was, then asked if he knew what his friend Hamid Abu Hamid had done in the fighting the night before; and when Abd al-Karim said he hadn't, Mansour went on to give him a brief account.

✖

The night before Abu Hamid had fought with the enemy. Hiding in the fields, he'd ambushed a group of them creeping up from the direction of the lake to make a breach in the defenses, and shot at them with his rapid-firing machine gun.

Some had fallen and the rest fled, but he'd waited for a while, fearing trickery from the ones on the ground, afraid they were waiting for the chance to open fire at him. The crops were over a foot high, waving in the breeze. The men with the Bren gun on top of the station had promised to give him any cover he needed, so he didn't feel afraid, just wary, considering calmly what to do.

The fallen men were just a few yards away, eight or nine strides perhaps. He picked up some pebbles and threw them toward them, then looked back, but could see only the outlines of some houses and the station. There was a slight movement among the crops. Fear gripped him and his heart missed a beat. His fingers were tense on the trigger.

Should he fire or not? Had it been the footfall of a soldier, or just a field mouse leaving its hole, or some dried-up fruit dropping on the ground? He waited, hardly daring to breathe. Another group, it occurred to him, might be following the first one. He thought of their barrels opening fire.

The ears of grain swayed on in the wind, and the mellow smell of the crops filled his nostrils. He took a deep breath. Still he waited, on and on, hearing no further sound. Then he started crawling cautiously, moving his gun from arm to arm, crawling toward them, in the grip of the courage that fills people at moments of life and death.

If he fell a martyr, he wondered momentarily, would anybody in Samakh know of his courage? He reflected for a moment, then stopped.

There was a body there – one body. The others must have crept away. Just one body – of a soldier who hadn't had time to fire a single bullet. It was just sprawled across the crops.

He stopped, taken by surprise. Was he really the one who'd done this? He couldn't see the soldier's face and he didn't want to. He prodded him with his foot. The man was stone dead, his rifle by his side. He stripped him of his cartridge pouch, took his rifle, then made his decision and started crawling back, on his stomach, over the soil and stones. He was exhausted now, his muscles twitching, and when he stopped to rest, the scent of grass and dew and wild flowers met him once more.

He raised his head. It wasn't far now. Dawn was near and the fighting was less fierce. The sky announced the coming daybreak. Suddenly he thought of his yellow car. He looked back, every sense on the alert, but couldn't see a thing through the mist.

The Jews must have failed to break through and fallen back. There was no shooting at all now on this part of the front. Best to take a rest, he thought, till dawn broke; otherwise he might be shot at by mistake, from the front positions behind the rail tracks.

When he heard Abu Adnan al-Zabadneh uttering the dawn call to prayer, a sense of safety descended on him. He remembered his wife, and he remembered the baby girl, feeling a desire to see her. He leaped to his feet and strode along, carrying his rifle.

Soon he was approaching the station. He could see them now, and they'd spotted him too. Mansour had picked him out with his binoculars, and now he was standing with the others at the entrance to the station, whose tiled roof had been destroyed. They rushed forward to meet him.

When he'd reached the station, he sat down on the concrete wall, and all eyes were on the strange rifle he was carrying along

with his own automatic. Then he asked for a glass of water, and drank enough to slake his thirst. The men had been fighting all night, engaging the enemy from near or far. After his drink Abu Hamid realized he'd broken through the barrier of fear. When he'd leaped over the fence and advanced to meet the enemy, God had granted his heart courage and daring. And now Mansour was standing in front of him, talking of the strength and boldness he'd shown. One of the men was examining the rifle.

"It's British-made," he said. "A sniper gun maybe. A Lewis gun."

They inspected it with interest, while he looked at the binoculars hanging on Mansour's chest. Suddenly an idea struck him. He jumped up, took the binoculars from around Mansour's neck and climbed up onto the roof, bare now, its covering of tiles destroyed.

He planted his feet firmly, fearful of slipping, and raised the glasses, scanning the far distance in the direction of the yellow car. But there was no yellow Ford there. It had disappeared. Over the fields he saw convoys of military vehicles, crossing the road that linked Tiberias with the settlements along the Beisan road. The stream was endless.

✖

"People are leaving the town," Hafiza said. "What are you going to do?"

Haj Hussein thought for a moment.

"If things get much worse," he said, "we could move the women and children, and the old people, to the outlying areas. To al-Hawi, maybe, or Tellat al-Duwair, or al-Tawafiq, or even al-Hammeh."

Then, looking up at her, he said:

"We must hold out for another two weeks, Hafiza, until the Arab armies come."

Hafiza was brave and stout-hearted, but she knew well enough that, with Tiberias fallen, the road to Samakh was open.

"You really think you can hold them off?" she asked. "Until the Arab armies arrive?"

They were there alone in the reception room, and he'd poured himself a cup of bitter coffee which made the bitter taste in his mouth stronger still.

"I just don't know," he said.

Life outside was in turmoil too. The whole rhythm of the town had changed. People passed by with hurrying steps, and the refugees who'd come to Samakh from Tiberias had started moving on to al-Hammeh and al-Adsiyyeh, even east to Jordan. The cows and other animals roamed about among the houses, because the shepherds and herdsmen hadn't come to take them out to pasture.

Abu Hamid got home to find his wife washing the baby's diapers. The baby herself was lying on the sheepskin close by, playing with her hands, her cheeks rosy now. The woman wiped the water from her arms and stood up.

"What's that?" she asked, indicating the weapon on his shoulder, the Lewis gun that looked so new and shiny, quite unlike the rusty old Sten gun.

"We won it in the battle," he answered shortly.

A rare smile, a smile of joy, lit up her worn face. He asked in his turn:

"How's the baby?"

"May God ward off the evil eye—she's like Jubaina in the fairy stories. God bless you for bringing us this little baby." Then, for the first time, she thought to ask: "What's happened to the car?"

"God will repay us," he said. "Are we to cry over a car, when the whole country's being lost?"

He thrust his hand in his pocket, feeling the beaded chain the car keys hung from, and fingered the keys with the sense of losing a friend, of someone with a living, beating heart, rather than mere pieces of metal. His wife took a step forward.

"People have started talking of leaving," she said. "To go somewhere safe."

He wasn't listening. He was gazing at the playing baby, at its innocent face. He remembered the white headscarf borne from beyond the wind, then caught on the thorns of a bramble bush, and felt fear of an unknown disaster that might strike anyone, at any moment.

"Come on," she said. "What are we going to do? Do we have to stay until the Jews slit our bellies open?"

To get away from her question, he went on through to the next room, to be alone for a while. There, his eyes fell once more on the picture of the Mufti that was hanging on the wall. A slight smile was drawn on his lips. He thought: do you see, Your Eminence the Mufti? We'll fight, Your Eminence, but the Jews are armed to the teeth. If only you could send us a battalion of fighters – if you could only send us three mortar guns, and send us al-Taher with his brothers from the sabotage group. Things are desperate, Your Eminence. Lend us your aid.

Chapter Thirteen

From the account of Abd al-Rahman the Iraqi

Events followed one another endlessly, as though there were some race to find catastrophe and misfortune. Disasters came on the heels of disasters, calamities rained from on high or sprang up from the depths of the earth. Towns and villages started falling to the enemy, and troops thronged the approach to the Holy City.

We were on maximum alert, the bitter taste of evil news in our mouths once more. Everyone knew now that our armies were short of weapons and ammunition and money. We moved to a new position, our small force joining a larger grouping based at the village of al-Nabi Samuel.

Asad al-Shahba had regained his composure. He'd stopped recounting his memories now, breathing not a word about Malak or her lost brother. All his thoughts were reserved for hearing the news on the radio and reading the daily newspapers that reached us from Jerusalem.

One evening the unit commander, Colonel Nour al-Din, came and told us of orders to move to the village of Beit Nuba, where we were to take part in a battle to stop the Jews from reaching Jerusalem.

He was dressed in his smart military uniform, and the next day, before we left, he popped in wearing the bullet-proof vest over it—that same wonderful vest that had almost cast a spell over our friend Najib.

✖

Then, to our amazement, Najib suddenly reappeared, after the battle of Bab al-Wad in which we'd fought. The Jewish forces had occupied the area of Beit Mahsir and the other heights overlooking Bab al-Wad, and now they were threatening Jerusalem. They'd got hold of new field cannons, and their bulldozers were cutting a path through the wild hills.

Our assault started at four o'clock in the morning on the eleventh of May. The platoons attacked, the guns opened fire and the infantry fought hand to hand with the Jews. Then extra troops came to reinforce us and support our position. The mountain battle went on for six hours, and in the end the enemy was defeated, with our forces gaining control of all the positions they'd occupied in the hills and the forest.

We'd regained the Beit Mahsir area, and the place was strewn with the bodies of Jewish soldiers, along with their burnt and damaged armored cars and weapons. On our side too a number of martyrs had fallen, among them Colonel Nour al-Din himself. We'd found him with a bullet hole through his head, from a large gun, behind a forward trench at Khirbet Harsis. The bullet had entered his forehead and torn the skull apart. He'd fallen during the final stages of the battle.

He'd shown courage, that elegant man, fighting fiercely in his bullet-proof vest. But the vest hadn't saved him. I took one final look at him as they carried him off to the ambulance, a lifeless body. They weren't even bothering to take off the vest—no one cared. They just took him and that was that.

When the shooting finally stopped, and we were in control of the front, our various advancing forces met up, and it was then that Najib suddenly appeared, riding in an armored car. He was looking out over its turret, manning the automatic gun.

When he saw me, he waved, then leaped off the top in a single bound and stood there in front of me. We embraced, then talked for a while. I asked how things were going with him, but his answers were brief, because he had to get back to his armored car. We met again, though, a few days later, after we'd turned over our positions to forces from the regular Arab armies.

It was in Jericho we met, at a mass troop camp, and he was with Ahmad Bey, who grasped our hands and once again called us his sons. He was a weary man, who deserved sympathy and perhaps some pity, too. He went to the tent assigned to him and fell fast asleep.

As for Najib and Asad al-Shahba and me, we took the chance to go off into town, where we spent the evening in a café under the palm trees, and Najib gave brief answers to our questions, using the sort of language they use in telegrams. He'd gone into Jerusalem, he told us, to look for a fellow townsman from Samakh, an officer in the Mufti's forces, but hadn't found him. The man had apparently gone on a mission behind enemy lines.

After many days of hanging around, Najib had joined an army force stationed at Beit Surik. The force's commander was in such desperate need of fighters he'd taken him immediately, without waiting for approval from the High Command. Najib told us of his emotions when he heard how Tiberias had fallen, then Samakh, with so many other towns and villages following.

He had no news of his townspeople from Samakh, the people he'd lived among. He didn't make any special mention, either, of his divorced wife, Badriyyeh, but you could see in his eyes that, deep down, the *muknissat al-janna* was still with him.

✖

A few days later we left too, as part of a huge convoy moving from Jericho to Amman. We slept one night on the outskirts of the Jordanian capital, then moved on to Damascus and from there to our old camp at Dumair.

When the Arab expeditionary forces reached Palestine, talk of it was on everyone's tongue, but the news from the first battles didn't bode well. As for us, there were rumors flying around the camp that our role was over, that the Inspector-General had issued the order for half the forces to be demobilized and the other half attached to the regular armies. We didn't take the rumors seriously at first, but it became clear, later, that they were true.

The demobilization lists started arriving in batches, and the camp got emptier and emptier; then, after quite a few weeks, the lists started hovering over us. Asad al-Shahba's order was the first, and, though Ahmad Bey intervened in person to try and reverse it, we all found ourselves demobilized within the week. Ahmad Bey came in scowling, along with a non-commissioned officer who was holding a list of ten names. It didn't take a genius to know it was our turn now.

Ahmad Bey didn't ask us to hand in our papers and take our honorable discharges. He just said: "There's no place for any of us in this army now. Come on, pack up your things. They don't need us any more."

We put on our civilian clothes, then, carrying our small cases, we climbed onto a transport vehicle that approached al-Guta along the desert road, then turned toward it and, passing among verdant trees, entered the city from Bab Tuma and finally came to a halt in Marjeh Square. It was noon, and there were ten of us in the back. None of us talked. Each of us was living out his own particular exile, on his own island, following his own thoughts wherever they led. Just imagine how we felt at that moment. Sorrow and dejection, agony and suppressed fury, all mixed together.

So, the vehicle stopped in Marjeh square, and Ahmad Bey,

who'd been sitting in front next to the driver, got out. He was carrying a small case too, and, without waiting for us to get out, he waved his hand and said tearfully:

"Goodbye, all of you."

We scrambled down from the back, but he didn't stop, and we saw him moving further and further off, carrying his small case, until he was swallowed up in the crowds. As for the driver, he just moved on without a word. Maybe he was used to this job now, and nothing surprised him any more.

We all shrugged and said our farewells, then each man went his own way. There were just the three of us left, standing by the fountain which, for some reason, wasn't working that day. Najib didn't say anything, still shocked by the whole thing, even if it hadn't come as a complete surprise.

I suggested going to a nearby café, and we picked up our cases and crossed to the opposite pavement and sat down there. Nobody felt much like talking. We drank some cups of coffee and watched the bustle of the street, and secretly I envied those people, walking by in pursuit of their particular goals. Where were we to go? And what were we supposed to do?

Tears were welling up in Asad al-Shahba's eyes, blotting out the nights of bombardment, the dust storms, the glitter of medals and the fall of cities. Najib came briefly out of his silence and said:

"I must go and look for them."

He didn't say who, but it was obvious enough. Who could they be but what was left of his family and the people from his home town, Samakh? I backed him up, and suggested Asad al-Shahba should go to his uncle's house and ask about Malak, and about the boy who'd been lost, swallowed up among the lanes and alleyways. Had he maybe come back now?

The tears in Asad al-Shahba's eyes kept welling up, setting a veil over the song of the nightingale perched on the pomegranate tree, and the music of the brass band at Colonel Ma'moun's funeral, and the patch of blood on that bullet-proof vest. I pressed his hand, understanding the turmoil deep inside him.

So was this the end of our quest? The end of our dreams of glory, of medals and heroism, to be flung down now by the wayside? I remembered the desert I'd crossed a few months before, and I remembered my mother. I remembered my uncle al-Hajji too, and the grains of sand, the howling of the wolves, the songs of joy at approaching battles, the dawn with its pale white hue, the breeze bringing tears to the eyes.

"Well," I said, doing my best to sound casual, "we did our duty anyway. Come on, let's go and find something to eat."

"I don't feel like eating," Najib muttered.

A woman was passing in front of us, wrapped in a cloak, but her palms weren't dyed with henna. Asad al-Shahba didn't even notice. The tears in his eyes were hiding the songs of the fire that burns on the mountain tops.

"I must go and look for them," Najib repeated.

I pressed Asad al-Shahba's hand again.

"Go on," I urged him. "Go back to your uncle's house, and I'll go with Najib. We'll be back soon, you can count on that. We'll meet again."

Asad al-Shahba started sobbing. Then, when he'd calmed down, he went with us to the stop for the buses to Deraa. He promised to go straight to his uncle's house, then described his father's restaurant in Aleppo, and insisted I go there just as soon as I could make it.

He stood and waited there with us with his case, not wanting to leave us, the desperate loneliness visible in his eyes. As the bus moved off, he waved from the pavement, then turned around sharply, as though to hide the flood of emotions on his face.

✖

As for us, we sat in the back of the crowded bus, side by side. As it moved off, Najib turned to face the window, and I respected his silence, leaving him to his reflections. I closed my eyes and tried to sleep, but I couldn't drop off. Then I tried to look out of the window, but that was no good either.

We passed through a lot of villages – al-Kiswa, Utman, al-Sheikh Miskeen – and as we moved on through open spaces, and past trees and black stone houses, I recalled the first time we'd traveled this road on our way to Palestine through Jordan. We'd been fairly bursting with enthusiasm then, and as we went on toward Deraa there'd been men waving to us from behind their plows and from the roofs of their houses, while the Hourani peasant women ululated at the top of their voices.

We'd been burning with joy then, all singing together. The eagerness had passed from throats to palms, and the dawn that day really had been one of a pearly white hue. Asad al-Shahba had been overcome by the awe of those long-awaited moments, thinking deep thoughts of the flaming horizon and the banner waving beyond the smoke. How I felt for Asad al-Shahba, left alone there now. My heart was totally with him.

May your spirit find repose and your heart peace, you brave fighter and fine man. Go to your beloved with the henna-dyed palms, and let her restore your broken soul and clean your wounds. May a smile find its way to your lips again, and may you find joy in your path. May jasmine, basil and mint fill your days with fragrance.

✖

We got off at the bus station in Deraa, amid an unusual bustle of coming and going; there were some looking for their people, others waiting for the missing to return. There was a flow of carts piled high, and a few possessions carried on heads. There were barefoot women and children, and the tragedy was etched on every face. The town had been inundated by a human flood of refugees fleeing massacres, flowing on unabated from the entrance of al-Hammeh to Quneitra, and on to Deraa – a flood that enveloped the town in an atmosphere of disaster. The pavements were thronged, the faces blank with shock, and nothing was as it should have been. We cut through the crowds, then Najib stood there on the pavement, staring into people's faces, examining them in the hope of maybe spotting someone he knew.

And he actually did find an old man from his home town. He greeted him and kissed him, then started asking what had happened; but the old man's answers were brief. He asked about the people of the town. I didn't hear the old man's reply, but Najib enlightened me as we moved on.

"They were scattered along the way," he said. "Some came to Quneitra and others crossed over the river into Jordan."

Not having any identity cards, we took the smugglers' road into Jordan, crossing valleys and mountains and, when night fell, staying along with the bedouins and shepherds, sharing their simple food and sleeping deep in a big cave where the shepherds slept with their flocks. The smell of the animals reminded me of that hard journey when I'd crossed the Syrian desert from Baghdad to Damascus.

Early next morning we drank some milk, then went on through the valleys to the village of al-Mukhaiba, opposite al-Hammeh, where so many refugees had gathered. We got there, finally, after a whole day's slog, in which our only companions had been the countryside, the silence, and birds floating in the blue of the sky. The region was a desolate one, the valleys deep, the plains stretching out endlessly, and beyond the heights were further heights.

Still we walked, on and on, plotting our course from the sun, and from the shadows cast by the trees. Sometimes we talked as we went, sometimes we walked in silence.

At sunset we looked around for some means of direction, not wanting to stop, but the sky gave us no sign. Then we smelled sulphur borne on the hot air, coming from beyond the next bend, and we knew we were almost there.

And so we went on to the village of al-Mukhaiba, whose occasional lights were there in front of us. The pain, which I'd had to put up with until now, started tearing at the ligaments of my legs. As we approached, the dogs started barking among the scattered houses and the banana groves by the river. Then a pack of them came racing at us, barking so fiercely I thought their small heads would burst. A man came out from the banana thickets, with a stout stick in one hand and a lantern in the other.

"Who's there?" he shouted.

When we'd reassured him, he silenced the dogs and invited us into his hut there in the midst of the banana grove. He was a good man, with a swarthy face and white hair. He didn't ask who we were or what we wanted. He simply motioned to us to sit down, and offered us the dates and rye bread he had.

Before he'd taken a single bite Najib started asking him anxiously about the people of Samakh. The man nodded.

"Yes," he said, "they did pass through here."

He launched into a description of the columns of refugees fleeing Tiberias, Samakh, al-Sahra, al-Ubaidiyyeh, Nasser al-Din, Loubia and al-Shajara. Then, pausing to light a cigarette, he added:

"They came through quickly, though. They were afraid of the malaria you get here this time of the year."

Najib asked if there were any still around there.

"There are a few down by the river," the man answered. "All that will be easier in the morning."

And with that he stretched out on an old rug, obviously wanting to sleep.

We slept too—or rather tried to. The moment we put out the light, the mosquitos attacked us, swarms of them, relentlessly sinking their needles in our skin. We tried to fight them off, but it was no use, and in the end our exhaustion got the better of us and we sank into sleep.

✖

Mosquitos and the disaster. The savage, bloodsucking mosquitos, with malaria in their sting, swarmed in the sky while the disaster swept along streets and squares and forsaken paths. Next morning we moved among the groups of refugees crossing the river into Jordan; among wan faces with dead eyes, faces drained by shock.

There were mothers trying to nurse from breasts where the milk had dried up, and pale-faced men carrying children too exhausted to walk any further; people waiting for their families, suitcases, bundles and abandoned possessions, all amid a clamor shot through with the sounds of lamentation.

By the side of the river, at the crossing point where the columns were passing, Najib found someone he knew. They embraced warmly, then both burst into tears. The man was wearing a navy blue uniform with brass buttons, and his face was etched deep with sorrow. Najib introduced him to me.

"This is Mansour," he said. "He was the ticket seller at the train station back home."

We sat down near the hot springs, whose steam smelled strongly of sulphur, and the man took a pack of cigarettes from his pocket and lit one. You could see the mosquito bites on his hands and neck and above his brows. As the two of them talked on, I took the chance to go to one of the springs, to try and get some relief from the pain in my legs. When I got back, Najib said:

"We have to move on."

"Where to?"

He pointed to the heights behind us.

"To the Umm Qais mountains," he said. "Or else Irbid. As for Mansour," he went on, turning to him, "he's going back to al-Hammeh, and he'll take the train to Deraa. He doesn't feel like living in a town with no trains."

We said goodbye to Mansour and stood watching as he went off.

"All he'll find is the way to loss and exile," Najib said. "He came with a group from Samakh. They've decided to move on east, but he'd rather go north."

I wanted to ask Najib if he'd had any news of Badriyyeh, the woman he always saw in his dreams watering the *muknissat al-janna,* but I held back. I knew there was no place for dreams any more, in this bitter reality.

So our next stop was to be the heights of Umm al-Qais, where, Najib told me, he'd find the family of Haj Hussein. There he'd learn all the news, and work out what to do about his own future.

As for me, I thought of returning to Baghdad. But I didn't feel inclined to go back there, carrying the smell of defeat and disaster on my clothes. Instead, I thought, I'd stay with Najib—after all, I'd tied my destiny to the destiny of these people, who'd lost their homes and their towns and villages.

The road was a long one, winding upward, empty even of shepherds and peasants. We walked for a whole day, and, just before sunset, began to approach the village of Umm al-Qais, with the borders of the lake starting to come into view on the other side.

Najib stopped under an ancient carob tree and looked out at the sunset and its reflection in the lake, breathing in the smell of Samakh. Many months had passed since he'd smelled Samakh's soil and water, but it had been fertile in his dreams and waking hours alike.

Suddenly he started talking in a high voice—but it wasn't me he was addressing. He was talking to people he could see but I couldn't, to men and women, and to trees and horses too, in words that were tender, simple and almost broke my heart. He talked with the goldfinch and the lark and the wild quail. He addressed the fennel and the vetch, the *marar* and the wild mint.

He talked to the surface of the lake, that was like the underbelly of a doe, and the *musht* fish, the *karseen*, the *athathi*, the *balbout* and the *marmour* fish.

I pressed his hand to draw him out of his reverie, and he walked on, still talking.

We climbed on upward, with the lake, to one side of us, getting bigger all the time. When we reached the peak on the outskirts of Umm al-Qais, the sun finally set and Najib once more came to a stop, and started talking to things only he could see. Then he let out a bitter sigh, and the tears flowed from his eyes.

I realized then that everything had been lost, and that all paths led to exile and dispersion. Such a melancholy prospect. Such a lonely road.

The End

About the Translators

MAY JAYYUSI was born in Amman, Jordan to Palestinian parents, and was educated at London University and Boston University. She is a PROTA reader and translator, and has worked extensively selecting poetry and fiction translated by PROTA. She has translated Ghassan Kanafani's *All That's Left to You and Other Stories* (1990), Zayd Mutee' Dammaj's novel *The Hostage*, and a collection of the poetry of Muhammad al-Maghut, *The Fan of the Swords* (1991). She lives with her husband and two children in Jerusalem.

CHRISTOPHER TINGLEY was born in Brighton, England and was educated at the universities of London and Leeds. Following initial teaching experience in Germany and Britain, he lectured in the fields of English Language and Linguistics at the University of Constantine, Algeria, the National University of Rwanda and the University of Ouagadougou, Burkina Faso. In the field of translation, he collaborated with the author on the translation of the extracts of Arabic poetry in S. K. Jayyusi's two volume work *Trends and Movements in Modern Arabic Poetry*; he has also co-translated (with Olive and Lorne Kenny as first translators) Yusuf al-Qaid's novel, *War in the Land of Egypt, The Hostage,* and many short stories.

Unequal Conflict
The Palestinians and Israel
by John Gee

Unequal Conflict re-examines Israel's apparent victory "against the odds" and argues that the odds in fact were always stacked in Israel's favor. As a phase of modern Palestinian history draws to a close in defeat, what can be salvaged? Is Palestine doomed, or can it be transformed and revitalized? These fundamental questions frame this stimulating and original account.

ISBN 1-56656-303-8 • $15.00 pb • 160 pages

Middle East Conflicts
by François Massoulié

The post-World War I colonial division of the Arab world stands at the root of many of today's conflicts. From Syria and Lebanon to Iraq and Kuwait, states were established with arbitrary borders that continue to spark conflicts. The establishment of Israel one world war later and the expulsion of hundreds of thousands of Palestinian Arabs from their ancestral homes set the stage for a continuing region-wide cycle of occupation and resistance.

ISBN 1-56656-237-6 • $15.00 pb • 160 pages • color photos & maps

Original Sins
Reflections on the History of Zionism and Israel
by Benjamin Beit-Hallahmi

"*Original Sins* is thought -provoking and valuable... [It] is brilliant in its overall anlysis... Beit-Hallahmi succeeds in presenting a wide-ranging yet concise, highly readable, well-organized, rational analysis that is laced with fresh insights and hard-hitting criticisms. *Original sins* is to date the best brief overview published in English of the definition and history of Zionism in theory and practice."
—Middle East Policy

ISBN 1-56656-130-2 • $29.95 hb
ISBN 1-56656-131-0 • $14.95 pb • 232 pages

Sharing the Promised Land
A Tale of Israelis and Palestinians
by Dilip Hiro

"[A] clear, non-judgemental and unbiased account of Israeli-Palestinian relations... Every aspect of the conflict is given a refreshing airing..."
—Jerusalem Post

Indian-born Dilip Hiro, one of the most experienced of Middle East hands, provides readers with a comprehensive chronicle of Israeli and Palestinian lives, shaped by negotiation and confrontation, right up to the present.

ISBN 1-56656-320-8 • $45.00 hb
ISBN 1-56656-319-4 • $18.95 pb • 320 pages